THE TOUCH
OF A
V¡LLA¡N

THE BOYS OF CLERMONT BAY

HOLLY RENEE

The Touch of a Villain
Cover Model: Sergio Carvajal
Cover Designer: Cassie Chapman with Opulent Designs
Editor: Becca Mysoor and Ellie McLove
Proofread: Rumi Khan
www.authorhollyrenee.com

for Christina

FOR ALWAYS BELIEVING
IN ME WHEN I DON'T
BELIEVE IN MYSELF.

I'M SO THANKFUL FOR
YOU.

THE TOUCH
OF A
VILLAIN

CHAPTER ONE

JOSIE

I never wanted this. Life wasn't supposed to go like this.

I picked up a shell out of the sand and almost crushed it in my hand before I threw it. It disappeared into the dark water, and I knew I would never see it again.

Just like I would never see my mom.

"What did the ocean ever do to you?"

I jolted at the sound of the voice from behind me and spun around. There was little light out on the beach except for what came from the house party and the steady beam of the moon, and I could barely make him out as he made his way toward me.

The ocean hadn't done anything to me.

"Nothing." I shook my head and looked back out toward the ocean as he sat down in the damp sand a couple of feet away from me.

The ocean hadn't done a thing but be steady and constant and infuriating. It was a reminder of how vast the world was, and of how alone I was in it.

My mom was gone, and my dad didn't care.

And my new stepbrother had lost me the moment we arrived at this stupid party.

I had barely known him a week, and already, he felt as unreliable as the rest.

I was alone and the ocean mocked me.

He leaned back on his elbows, and I couldn't stop myself from peering over at him. He looked like he belonged out here on this beach. His skin was tan and his dark hair flopped forward into his face, making my hands itch to touch it even though I didn't know him.

"I'm Beck." He leaned on his elbow and held his hand out to me. I stared at his hand for a second before placing my own in his.

"Josie."

He dropped my hand and a wicked grin lit up his face.

I knew that this boy was trouble. Even with only knowing his name, I knew that. That fact was easy to spot from a mile away.

"You new here?"

"I am."

"And you're already over the party?" He hiked his thumb over his shoulder toward the still pumping music.

"Guilty."

He smiled again, but I had no idea what the hell he was smiling about.

"Why aren't you in there?" I let my gaze run over his full lips to his sharp jaw. He was handsome in a way that made me feel like I shouldn't be looking at him. Like he was a sin.

"I'm over it too." He looked like he meant it. Whatever was going on at the party, he had as little interest in returning as I did. "You want to go somewhere?"

My body tensed at his words. I didn't even know this guy, and he wanted me to go somewhere with him?

Silence lingered in the air between us. A smirk sliced through his lips and a mischievous look rolled through his eyes as they held my attention. Yeah, this guy was trouble, and for some crazy reason, he intrigued me. He held up his hands, his smirk deepening. "I didn't mean it like that. There's just this really cool spot a little way down the beach. You can either stay here and throw some more shells or you can trust a stranger. Choice is yours."

I should have said no. I had seen enough true crime documentaries to have that instilled in my head, but part of me wanted to go with him. There was no way in hell I was going back into that party that was more orgy than truth or dare, and I had my cell phone in my back pocket.

I glanced at the extravagant house before looking back at him. I was sure there were worse ways to die.

"Are you going to murder me?"

A loud, boisterous laugh shot from his lips. "I don't think so."

"Have you ever murdered anyone else before?"

His eyes sparkled, and I couldn't tell if they were brown or green or a mix of the two colors, but I knew they were mesmerizing.

"If I had, do you think I would be sitting here on the beach with you?"

"Probably." He stood and dusted the sand off of his jeans.

"It's a well-known fact that attractive serial killers get away with their crimes for a lot longer."

He cocked his head to the side and ran his teeth over his bottom lip as he ran his gaze over every part of me. "You think I'm attractive?"

Shit. Did I say that out loud?

"We both know you're attractive." I rolled my eyes and stood alongside him. My blue jean shorts were damp from the sand, but I dusted them off the best I could. "The unknown factor here is if you're innocent or on the run."

His smile turned devilishly lethal with the deepening of his grin.

"So, are you going to chance it?" His voice was as smooth as butter as he took a step back, and I found myself eager to follow him.

I knew I was going to say yes before the word ever left my lips. I was in this town all alone. In this world all alone, and I desperately wanted to be anywhere other than where I was.

I didn't want to think about my dad or my stepbrother or the fact that I could no longer turn to my mom.

I wanted to take a risk with him regardless of the consequences.

No one would even notice if I was gone. I doubted they would even care.

I was on my own, and the only thing that mattered in that moment was the two of us on this beach with no one to stop us.

No one to care about the reckless decisions I made.

I took a step past him and looked him over. "I don't even know you." I didn't wait for him as I kept walking in the direction he was heading, but he quickly caught up.

"You can get to know me." He got ahead of me and turned around to face me. His eyes trailed over me from head to toe as he walked backward in the sand, and I couldn't help but notice that his gaze held no shame when it finally met mine again. "We can play a game."

"A game?" My stomach tightened as I thought about the kind of games he probably played. His eyes sparked with mischief, as if daring me to take a risk.

"Yes. You can make an assumption about me, and I'll let you know if it's true, then I can make one about you."

This game of his sounded dangerous, but I had already made plenty of assumptions about him in my head.

"You're a player."

He rubbed his chest playfully, but his eyes lit up at my words. "Damn. Right off the bat, huh?"

I couldn't help but laugh. "Am I wrong?"

"You're not right." He shifted to walking beside me, and the smell of him overwhelmed me.

His cologne was a mixture of smoke and spice, and I could practically taste it on my tongue. "But you're not completely wrong."

He smiled before biting down on his bottom lip. "My turn. You're an only child."

"Yes." He technically wasn't wrong. Lucas was only my stepbrother, and I wasn't meeting him until after I was seventeen. In every way that mattered, I was an only child.

He snapped his fingers. "One for one."

We walked farther down the beach, and I thought about

what to say next. I had plenty of assumptions about him in my mind, but I wasn't sure that I should say any of them out loud. "You're not an only child."

"I'm not. I have a younger sister."

"Poor thing." I chuckled. "I bet she can never get a date with you around."

A storm brewed in his eyes before he pulled his gaze away from me and out toward the ocean. I instantly regretted what I had said.

"I shouldn't have said that."

He grinned and slipped a mask over his emotions. "You're good. My turn."

I didn't push him further. I didn't even know this guy. I had no right to his secrets. Even if I desperately wanted to know them.

"I bet that you didn't want to move here."

"What makes you say that?" I crossed my arms. He was spot on.

"I don't know." He shook his head slightly. "I just get this feeling that you don't want to be here."

"I didn't really have a choice in the matter. No."

"It's not too bad." He kicked a small shell across the sand. "I've never lived anywhere else, but I don't hate it."

"Why do I get the feeling you can't wait to get out then?" We were still walking down the beach and passed more and more houses that looked so damn similar to the one we had just left. Some were larger than others, but they were all grandiose.

Just like my father's house. It was just up ahead.

"You're a little too good at this game." He chuckled and ran his fingers down the back of his neck. His bicep bunched under his t-shirt, and I saw the edge of a delicate tattoo peeking out. "I'm not leaving Clermont Bay."

"Like ever?" I laughed, but he looked serious.

"I mean, maybe eventually, but not anytime soon."

I understood how that felt. If it wasn't for my mother's life insurance policy, I wouldn't be able to pay for college either. Even with it, there was no way I would make it through without working my ass off. It didn't matter that my father had more money than I could ever dream of. I refused to touch any of it. "So, what? You just party with those rich assholes then?"

"Don't forget you were there too." He chuckled. "But unfortunately, I am one of those rich assholes." He pointed behind us to a house we had just passed. It only sat a few away from my father's, but it stood out from the rest. The large stone house looked like it had been there long before the rest of the homes even though it was still pristinely taken care of. It had a regal feel about it that made it seem old and established. Not like my father's. Everything about it felt new. "That's my house."

"That one?" I pointed at it in shock. I had no idea of Beck's last name, and I honestly didn't care to know. But I knew that whoever his father was, he had to be important to live in a home like that.

"That would be it."

"I can see why you don't plan on leaving."

He laughed and kept walking. We were passing my dad's house as we spoke, but I didn't point it out. There was a part of me that knew things may change between us if he knew who I was, if he knew who my dad was, and I didn't want that.

I knew I didn't want to run in the same crowd as Beck did. That party wasn't my scene, and it certainly wasn't a scene I wanted to be a part of. Plus, it was highly unlikely I would ever have another moment like this with Beck again, so I didn't want to taint it with information about my father.

"It's not that." He smiled, but this one didn't seem nearly as sincere as earlier. This was the fake Beck. This was the guy he put on for show. "I'm going to be helping my dad run his business."

"You're smiling, but you don't seem happy about that."

He chuckled, and it was like I could see his mask slipping firmer into place. "Isn't it my turn to make an assumption about you? I think we skipped my turn."

I waved my hand, telling him to go ahead. He took a moment to think, then snapped his fingers. "You, Josie... wait. What's your last name?"

"I'm not telling you."

"Why not?"

Because I don't want you to think differently of me. I don't want you to judge me solely based on who my family is.

"Because I don't know you." I laughed it off. "Next, you'll be asking me for my social security number."

He rolled his eyes, and the gesture was so cute on his handsome face.

"Fine. What about a middle name?"

"Rose." It was a middle name I shared with my mother and just saying it out loud made my chest ache. "What's yours?"

He winced just the slightest bit. "Eugene."

"Aw."

He pointed his finger so close to my face, and I immediately closed my mouth. "Do not say it's cute."

"But it is cute."

"Josie Rose, I think that you probably have a thing for jocks."

"Negative." I shook my head.

"Why not?"

"Umm, most jocks are douchebags." The beach curved to the right, and there was even less light the farther away we got from the party. I pulled out my cell phone and clicked on the screen.

I had one text from Lucas.

Where did you go?

I quickly responded to let him know I was on the beach as I listened to Beck talk.

"I take offense to that."

"So you're a rich boy and a jock?" I slid my phone back into my pocket.

"Does that mean I have two strikes against me?"

"Absolutely. You're walking a thin line here."

He chuckled and nudged my shoulder just as we made our way around the curve. I could barely see the beach behind us, but I wasn't looking there. I was looking at the giant rocks up ahead of us that formed into a cliff. The waves crashed violently against the rocks like they were angered by their mere existence, and it was so vastly different from the way they hit the beach.

It was absolutely breathtaking.

Beck pointed to a particularly dark spot among the rocks. "There's a small cave in the rock over there. We swim out and climb into it every summer."

"There's no way I'm going in there." I didn't think he was asking, but I wanted to make sure I was clear from the beginning. I had goose bumps just thinking about it. If the waves were that violent on the outside, I couldn't imagine what it would be like in there. Who knew what lurked in there?

I barely swam in the ocean. There was no way in hell I would purposely go into a cave.

He watched my facial expressions and laughed. "Even I'm not dumb enough to go into that cave in the middle of the night. Even though I'm a dumb jock."

"I didn't say jocks were dumb." The sand beneath our feet was changing over to small rocks, and I picked one up and attempted to skip it across the water and failed. "I called you all douchebags."

"Oh. Much better." He laughed. "I can tell you didn't grow up playing sports, your throw is weak as hell."

"Hey." I was actually offended by that.

"Here." He picked up another rock and placed it in my

hand. This one was much heavier than the last, but I barely noticed the weight as he moved behind me.

If I thought his smell was overwhelming before, it was suffocating now. But it was the most delicious suffocation. The ocean practically disappeared as I was consumed by him. His smell, his warmth at my back, his breath against my neck.

He lined his body up with mine, and he gently gripped my hand in his. I feared he could feel mine trembling, but if he noticed, he didn't say. He simply moved my arm back and forth as he talked.

"When you're trying to skip a rock, you have to throw it from the side." He showed me the movement again and again, but it wasn't registering. "You have to whip your wrist quickly and let the rock go at the perfect angle. The ocean really isn't the best place for this, though." He pressed his chest against my back and used it to turn my body in the correct angle. "You really need the water to be calm."

There wasn't a thing about me that was calm.

There wasn't a thing about me or the ocean that was calm.

"So there's no point to this?" I looked over my shoulder, and he was right there. His mouth was so close to mine. I would have to stand on my tiptoes to reach them, but I could do so easily. I could kiss him, and I knew I wouldn't regret a thing.

"There is definitely a point." His hand tightened around mine, and his gaze dropped to my lips.

He was going to kiss me. I didn't know anything about this boy or who he was or what he wanted, but I knew that. We didn't need to know anything about each other to know that I felt desperate for him to kiss me.

I licked my bottom lip, and he tracked the movement like a hunter.

"Josie!" I could hear my name being called in the distance, but I didn't care. I didn't want to end this moment, this trance I felt like I was under. I wanted Beck to kiss me before he thought better of it and turned away.

My name was called again in the distance, and Beck lifted his head toward the sound, but I was already moving. I let my hand fall from his, and I twisted against him as I wrapped my hand around his neck.

My heart was slamming against my chest, and my lungs felt like they were crashing into me with the same force of the ocean. I wasn't this girl. I didn't make bold moves or kiss a guy I didn't know.

But no one here knew who I was.

I was no one to them. A brand new face, a girl who was nothing but a mystery. I could be whoever I wanted to be here. I could create the girl I wanted them to know.

He looked back down at me, the sound forgotten, and he didn't wait for me to close the gap between us. He leaned down, the muscles of his neck straining beneath my fingers, and he pressed his lips to mine.

At first, it was gentle, his lips moved against mine, and I tried to breathe even though it felt impossible. Beck tugged my bottom lip with his teeth, and I couldn't hear a thing except for my harsh breath and the sound of his growl.

We didn't know each other, and somehow he wanted me as much as I wanted him. His hand pushed into the windblown strands of my hair, and he tilted my head backward just as his tongue hit mine. He tasted like wintergreen, and I couldn't get enough of him.

I chased his tongue with mine, and he tightened his hand in my hair. There was an edge of pain under his fingers, but I didn't care. It only made me want to get closer to him. We were practically surrounding each other, and still, I felt the urge to climb closer and closer until there wasn't a breath left between us.

I heard my name again, this time closer, but I still kissed

him. I didn't want to stop. I didn't want reality to hit and for him to remember that I was some stranger that didn't matter to him. I wanted to live in this moment, and I refused to allow anything to ruin it.

Even if it was just this one kiss, this one touch between us, it was perfect and messy. His teeth hit mine as he pulled me closer, and I clung to him as my lips moved faster and faster against his.

I had very little experience when it came to men, but I knew that this kiss wasn't a first kiss I would ever get again.

This would be it, then I would have to let it go. Beck would be the guy I compared other first kisses to for the rest of my life, and a twinge of fear ran through me at the thought.

He pulled away from me as my name was called again, and I bit down on his lip before slowly letting him go.

He lifted his head, but he was still staring down at me. I was wrong before. His eyes were much more golden than they were brown or green, and the moonlight seemed to flicker off the specks that I felt lost in.

Beck blinked away the fog that he had fallen under with me before turning toward the beach we had just come from only moments ago. I followed his gaze, and I didn't even have time to catch my breath before Lucas and some guy I didn't know came into view.

Beck's body went stock-still beside me and his hand slid from my hair. I quickly dropped mine away from him and stepped toward my stepbrother.

His face was flushed and his eyes looked murderous, but I had no idea what his problem was. I didn't even know the guy, despite his mother's marriage to my father, and he had no right to act like the protective older brother.

Even if he was technically about eight months older than me.

"What the fuck are you doing?"

"Calm down." I crossed my arms, but he wasn't talking to me. He and his anger were headed straight for Beck.

"What the fuck does it look like I'm doing?"

I spun around to face Beck. His voice sounded so different. He sounded so angry and irritated, and honestly, cold. Nothing like he was with me only moments before.

"Do you two know each other?" I looked back and forth between them, but neither one was looking at me. They were staring each other down in some sort of pissing contest, and I had no damn clue what the hell their problem was. "Hello."

"Yeah." Beck nodded and looked over at me. His eyes now felt as cold as his voice. I would have given anything to go back to being in his arms before Lucas interrupted us. I liked that Beck. That Beck felt intoxicating. This Beck was something different.

This Beck scared me a little.

"How do you know Lucas?"

I looked back between them because I was clearly missing something. "He's my stepbrother."

A harsh laugh fell from Beck's lips, and I watched as he clenched his hand at his side. Lucas moved toward me, and I jerked away from him as he reached out for my arm. I had no idea what was going on, but I didn't need him trying to be some knight in shining armor.

"Don't act like you didn't know who she was." The way Lucas said it made my gaze snap up to Beck. He knew who I was this entire time?

But Beck wasn't looking at Lucas anymore. He was glaring at me, and he no longer looked like he wanted any part of me. Those feelings washed out to sea the moment our kiss was over. The only thing Beck's face held now was pure disgust, and it was directed entirely at me. While his eyes glared, his mouth curled into an evil smirk. He looked like a threat no one would ever want.

He barely knew anything about me, but as soon as Lucas appeared and he learned of my connection to him, everything was forgotten and I became enemy number one.

He hated me. Instantly.

Whatever his reasoning was, Beck hated me and the way Lucas reached out for me again. He stared at his hand as if he could set it on fire with his stare. He was furious, and I had no idea what I had done.

"That's why you wouldn't tell me your last name." He laughed, and there wasn't an ounce of humor. "What did you do, Vos? Send your whore sister out here to seduce me?"

I jolted back as if he had slapped me. I felt his insult to my very core. Every part of me that felt alive under his kiss now felt like it was burning with embarrassment.

I had been such a damn fool.

"Fuck you, Clermont." Lucas pulled me closer to him, and I let him. I had no idea why he was so angry over me being out here with Beck. Why he was so protective.

Lucas barely knew me, but we were family. Even if we didn't know each other yet, he was all I had.

And he wanted me nowhere near Beck Clermont.

Clermont. Beck Clermont. As in Clermont Bay.

As in the family, this town and everything inside it was named after.

"Let's not compare whore sisters."

Beck lunged toward Lucas, but whoever the guy was that came with Lucas stepped in his way.

"Fucking move, Ben," Beck growled at him, but Ben stood his ground.

"That's not happening. We have summer training tomorrow."

I turned away from all of them and moved down the beach. I didn't want to hear another word of what either of them had to say. I felt so humiliated and dirty, and I wanted to get away from them as fast as I could.

I wanted to jump in the ocean and wash away his words and his touch and the way the taste of him still lingered in my mouth.

"Don't go near her again." Lucas was as mad as Beck, and I was suddenly thankful that he was here. Even if him being here had ruined everything, I didn't want to give Beck another second of myself.

He had more than I should have allowed already.

"I'll go near her if I want to." Beck's reply stopped me in my tracks. "There isn't a damn thing you can do to stop me. If I want to fuck her, I will."

I turned back to look at him. He was out of his damn mind.

"I could have fucked her right here on this beach if I had wanted to. I hadn't realized your sister would be as fucking desperate as you are."

I started toward him. I wanted to rage, to slam my fist against his chest, to demand he stop talking about me as if I wasn't right there, but Lucas was already beside me. He pulled me away from Beck and his evil fucking laugh that echoed behind me.

He was wrong. I would have never let him do that. I wasn't desperate or a whore, and I refused to be treated like one simply because I let some asshole kiss me on the beach. Because I had practically begged for it with my body.

"Fuck you, asshole," I yelled over Lucas's shoulder, and Beck's anger finally morphed into a smile. This one was nothing like the others he had given me earlier. Nothing about him was anything like that guy.

This was the real Beck Clermont, and I didn't like anything about him.

"I can't fucking wait, princess."

CHAPTER TWO

W hat the fuck was I thinking?

I had no idea who the hell she was when I stepped out onto the quiet beach. Parties in this town were shit most of the time, sometimes they served their purpose of getting laid, but if I turned up, it was for a reason. And when the people at these parties annoyed the hell out of me, I went to the beach. It was my place. My escape, my solitude, mine. The warm sand and damp ocean air. Mine. I had claimed it as my own long before she ever stepped foot on it, and now it was tainted with her.

The salty air reminded me of her hair whipping around in the strong breeze, the damn rocks made me crave the feeling of her hand in mine, and the spray of the ocean hitting my lips set my fucking soul on fire with thoughts of devouring that pretty little mouth of hers.

If I had known who she was, I would have sent her ass packing the moment I found her sitting there. If I had known she was related to that piece of shit, I wouldn't have given her a second glance.

But I hadn't known. And she was so damn gorgeous. Even in my anger, I could admit that. Her long brown hair was full and fell just below her breasts. Those were perfect too, along with her ass, but it was her deep brown eyes that I couldn't seem to forget.

There was a smattering of freckles across her nose that made her look so innocent. She looked so pure and sweet, and nothing like her fucking stepbrother. But the more I thought about it, the more I saw the similarities between her and her father.

I knew of Joseph Vos. Everyone in this town did, and I hated him as much as I hated his stepson.

And Jesus Christ, seeing Lucas act like he was some sort of fucking savior was beyond a joke. He was as far from a savior as I was a virgin.

The Lucas I knew was the most self-centered asshole. I hadn't realized that before, but I knew that now.

I knew that with a certainty that I wish I didn't.

The thought of him caring for her felt almost as shocking as knowing she was his sister. Lucas had never mentioned having a sister before, and I most certainly had not heard Mr. Vos talk of a daughter. I would have remembered it if I had.

I used to consider Lucas my friend, but just thinking of his betrayal made my stomach ache and my hands dig into my chair.

Josie was a Vos.

That was the only thing I needed to know.

It didn't matter that she was gorgeous or even a bit charming. It didn't matter that I had wanted to fuck her the moment her soft lips touched mine.

She had looked up at me like she wanted me, like she didn't even care or know who my family was, but that was all a lie.

The only look I cared about now was the one she had given me when she left. She was so angry, her face had fallen, and she looked like she hated me as much as I hated her.

Good.

I wanted her to hate me.

I wanted to ruin her and her smug fucking brother. But most of all, I wanted to ruin her damn father, who thought he was untouchable.

He was the one who kept Lucas protected from what he did. He had money and power, and he wielded it like a sword.

It didn't matter that my father had the same advantages. He would never allow me to get away with what Lucas had.

I looked over the people still drinking and trying to get laid, and I clicked on my phone. I searched her name on Instagram, and she quickly pulled up. She only had a few followers, and I found Lucas's name at the very top.

I clicked off her followers and scrolled through her photos.

She was gorgeous in all of them, and that only served to piss me off. There were no pictures of anyone else. Not Lucas, not her dad, not any sort of boyfriend.

"What was that about?" Cami sat down on my lap, and I quickly tucked my phone in my pocket.

"What?"

"That." She waved her hand toward the door Lucas had left through only moments before. I had followed him back to the house as he had stormed down the beach with Josie's hand in his. She had jerked her hand from his as soon as their house came back into view, and she disappeared through the gate as if she had never been there at all.

Lucas kept walking though. His expensive car and his stupid friends were still back at that party. But every bit of the party was forgotten to him as he jerked his keys from his pocket and stormed out the front.

I was thankful. I didn't have any more energy to give Lucas tonight.

He was pissed and everyone knew it, but I didn't give a shit what they knew. I didn't care if they thought I fucked his sister out on that dark beach like she was nothing but a whore.

Cami ran her fingers through my hair, and I pressed the back of my head against the chair and looked up at her. I used to feel something when I looked at her. There used to be a rush of attraction and the thrill of thinking about what she would do with her mouth.

But those feelings were gone. The urge to push her away from me was overwhelming.

"That girl." There was a tone of jealousy in her voice, but I knew it was all for show. Cami didn't care about me. She didn't care for much of anything but herself. But that wasn't really fair. She had cared for Frankie after everything happened. When no one else was there, she had been the one my sister could turn to.

Because Frankie had refused to turn to me.

"That's Lucas's sister."

Her eyes rounded in shock. "What?"

I tightened my hand around her waist and tried to make the feel of her body make me forget the feel of Josie's.

"I didn't know he had a sister."

"Neither did I."

Her gaze snapped to mine at my tone. Cami knew how much I hated Lucas. She knew what kind of toll it took on me to even be in the same room as him.

"What happened with her?"

"Nothing."

"It doesn't look like nothing."

My hand tightened further, and I wanted to throw Cami from my lap. She had no right to judge me or act like a jealous girlfriend. It didn't matter what anyone else thought or what we made them believe.

The two of us knew where we stood.

The two of us together had been unstoppable. No one ever fucked with us, but I still had the freedom to fuck whoever I wanted.

Cami pretended we were still more than what we were, and I let her. She used me to keep her freedom from her parents who would never approve of the real choices she was making, and I had used her to make my sister feel like she was alive again.

We had both needed each other once upon a time, and that need had morphed into something different. Cami was using me to hide her secrets, and I was now using her for her perfect pink mouth.

It was the best of both worlds for me. I got to be with Cami or any other girl I wanted, and no one had any real expectations from me. None of them were expecting a Prince Charming, thank fuck, because I wouldn't give that to any of them.

Not even Cami.

"Did something happen between you all?" She smiled as another girl walked by us and toyed with the chain around my neck.

"Nothing worth noting."

"So, I shouldn't be worried about this?" She leaned forward and pressed her lips to mine. "You're shaking, you're so angry."

She was right. I was. My grip on her and the arm of the couch was brutal and bruising, but I felt like I couldn't relax.

"I'm going to destroy her." I was honest with Cami for the first time in a long time.

"His sister?" She searched my eyes, and her blue ones didn't seem nearly as vibrant as they used to.

"It seems only fair, right?" I cocked my head and moved my hand farther up her side. Cami had the most amazing tits.

"This isn't a good idea." She shook her head, but she wouldn't be able to talk me out of it. I had stopped listening to what Cami said the moment I found out her secrets.

"I don't need your approval."

Her body jolted under my hand, and I knew that I had hurt her. But right now, I didn't care. "I know you don't."

She stood from my lap and reached her hand out for mine. "Let me take the edge off."

I thought about telling her no, but she was right. I needed this. I needed to stop thinking about Josie Vos and let Cami make me remember who I was.

I let her pull me into a bedroom, and I grinned as one of the guys catcalled. These people were far too easy to impress. They thought because I had Cami on my arm and in my bedroom, I was some sort of god.

I was a Clermont, and I was fucking the girl they all wanted, and they fucking worshipped me for it.

I closed the door behind me, and Cami dropped to her

knees. There was no build-up. No pretending this wasn't exactly what it was.

She opened the button of my jeans and pulled down my zipper with deft hands. Cami knew what she was doing, and I buried my hand in her hair as I watched her pull me into her mouth.

I was so fucking hard, and I couldn't control myself as I tightened my hands and slammed into the back of her throat. Her mouth felt so good, her lips wrapped perfectly around my cock, and she stared up at me in a way that used to fuel me.

But now all I could think about were those brown eyes of Josie's. I imagined what she would look like beneath me, how her hair would feel grasped in my hands. I slammed into her mouth over and over, and I didn't stop when her hands dug into my thighs or I felt the back of her throat spasm as she gagged.

I was already too far gone, and all I could see was her. Cami was the farthest thing from my mind, and I knew that should have made me feel guilty. But I had no room for guilt.

I was too overtaken with the urge to fuck Josie out of my mind. I wanted to destroy her and her family, and her daddy's perfect reputation. I wanted to make him feel what it was like to have someone else ruin something that belonged to you.

I wanted to tarnish her and mark her in a way that she would never forget.

She had just been a beautiful girl that I had found on the beach less than an hour ago, but she wasn't any of that now.

She was the girl I would ruin.

She had tasted so damn sweet out on that beach, but I knew it was all a lie. The taste of her, the feel of her under my fingers, the way she looked up at me like she had been craving my kiss as much as I had wanted hers.

She was nothing more than my revenge, and I came in Cami's mouth with her name on my lips.

CHAPTER THREE

It had been a week since I first arrived in Clermont Bay.

A week since my run-in with Beck.

That was what I was calling it. A run-in. I wouldn't give it any more power than that. Even though I had thought about it every single day.

Lucas huffed, and I looked over at him as he drove down the road that wound along the beach.

"What's wrong?" I had no idea why I asked because I already knew the answer. He was driving me to my first day at my new job, and he was one hundred percent against it.

Lucas and I had been spending time together over the past week, and I knew his feelings on the job.

"Nothing." He shook his head as the country club came into view.

I knew that he felt the same way my dad did about my job. Neither of them thought I needed to work, but I did.

I wasn't like Lucas.

I couldn't rely on my father.

Due to being my guardian and me being only seventeen, he held my mom's life insurance policy and our house until the day I turned eighteen, and as much as I wanted to allow myself to, I didn't trust him to take care of me. He didn't when I needed him before, and I knew I couldn't trust him to do so now.

And my father was a man who wielded his power like a weapon. I knew that from experience, and I couldn't imagine what he could do with the things that belonged to me.

I didn't want to be here forever. I wanted to leave this town and go back to Utah. I wanted to smell the warm vanilla of my mother's house, and stare at the bright yellow walls I didn't appreciate until now.

My heart ached just thinking about the house sitting there with no sounds of laughter echoing off the walls and none of the smells of my mother's chaotic cooking.

"I really wish you wouldn't work there." Lucas's hands tightened around the steering wheel. I knew that me getting a job at Clermont Bay Country Club really bothered him.

I wanted to ask him again what the problem was with him and Beck, but he had already told me before. I just couldn't imagine that the two of them hated each other that much over past conquests and competition in baseball.

That was what Lucas had told me, and I had no reason to question him.

But their hate was too strong, and I didn't understand it.

He hated Beck as if he had done something to ruin his life. He hated him as if he was his enemy.

But the country club was the only place that I put an application in that called me back, and trust me when I tell you that I put in a lot of applications.

I didn't want to work anywhere that was associated with Beck or his last name. But rich boys like him didn't hang around their daddies' businesses. He would be off doing things the same way Lucas was. Without a single thought of the future.

That was the thing about growing up with money. They didn't fear what was to come. They didn't fear what the future held for them. They had no reason to fear.

But I did.

I hadn't relied on my father's money my entire life.

And I wasn't going to start now.

"It's just a job, Lucas." I rolled my eyes. "I think I'll be fine."

"But you'll still be working for them."

I pushed my hair out of my face and fidgeted in my seat. Lucas drove a car that was a thousand times nicer than anything I had ever been in. Anything other than my father's. It only made the vast difference between us feel larger. "And I'm going to be a server. They won't even know I'm there."

No one would even look twice at me.

"I don't think you understand how badly Beck hates me."

"I will avoid Beck at all costs. Will that make you feel better?"

"Yes." He nodded his head, but his eyes darkened and I knew he wanted to say something more. There was something on the tip of his tongue, but I knew he was holding himself back. Whatever happened between him and Beck had affected him. "Just tell me if he bothers you again."

Technically, he hadn't bothered me the first time. Not until he found out who I was.

And if I did see him again, when I saw him again, I would meet him with a cold indifference.

I had let myself get carried away on that damn beach when the world had felt too heavy, but I wouldn't make that mistake again. Beck had made sure of that.

Whatever his intentions were, he had made sure to put me in my place. He had let me know exactly where I stood with him, and I wouldn't soon forget it.

I would never forget the way his hate for me had taken over every part of him. It was as if the boy in front of me had morphed into someone else completely, and I didn't like the one I saw.

The true Beck Clermont wasn't a guy I wanted anything to do with.

I would never allow him to touch me again. I didn't need Lucas or my father's warnings about him.

He had made sure I knew who he was himself.

He had made sure that I regretted every moment of that night.

And I did. I regretted every look, every touch, every damn way he had made me feel.

"He's not going to bother me." I had a feeling I would never hear from him again. "And if he does, I'll tell him to go to hell."

Even if the very idea of seeing him again made my pulse race and my stomach tighten in anticipation.

I didn't even know this guy, and he had me feeling like a mess.

I wouldn't subject myself to any more of him.

Even if he intrigued me.

Even if he was the most gorgeous guy I had ever laid eyes on.

He was an asshole, and I would rather never see him again.

"But if he does, you'll tell me." It wasn't a question. It was a demand. Lucas didn't want me anywhere near Beck, and I couldn't blame him.

"I promise."

We pulled into the country club, and I tried to take everything in.

The massive building was made of stone that was far older than I was, and for some reason, it reminded me of a castle. I had no doubt that the men inside ruled over it as if it were.

As if they were kings.

From the limited research I had been able to do about the club, I knew that it was exclusive. So exclusive that finding out any information about it on the internet was practically impossible.

And I had tried.

Lucas had been about as knowledgeable as old Google and as tight-lipped. The only helpful information he gave me was that our father was a member, and Beck's father owned the place.

Neither of those facts helped me.

I wasn't prepared for this.

I had never had a job like this before. Back home, I had been working at a local cafe to help my mom with the bills, but it was nothing of this caliber. I worked long, hard days, but my boss was nice, and the customers were familiar.

This place was anything but.

"I don't see his car." I brought my attention back to Lucas as he pulled his car in front of the building.

"Beck's?" I looked around, but I had no idea what he drove. I knew nothing about him outside of the fact that he tasted like wintergreen and he hated me.

"Yeah." Lucas's fingers tapped against the steering wheel. "He's not here."

"Okay." I nodded, and I felt a small amount of relief at his words. Running into Beck today would be my biggest fear. I needed this job and the security the money I could make here would provide, and I couldn't let some asshole take that away from me.

Climbing out of Lucas's car, I ran my hands down my mom's old black dress pants and tried to calm my racing heart.

These people were no better than I was.

"Good luck." Lucas sounded insincere, but I smiled at him before waving goodbye.

Regardless of what he and my father wanted, I was going to do this.

I had to.

I walked inside, the loud hustle and bustle of a kitchen hitting me the moment I passed through the door, and it calmed me somehow. I shifted out of the way as a server carrying a tray of clean glasses passed me, and I wondered where I was supposed to go. I peeked into the kitchen, the staff clearly setting up for the day, before I wandered farther to find the dining room.

Two men stood at the bar, looking over some paperwork, and I prayed that one of them was the Jack Smelcer I was supposed to be meeting.

That was the name human resources had given me.

Neither of them looked up as I approached, clearly wrapped up in whatever they were discussing, and I hated interrupting them. "Excuse me."

Both sets of eyes jumped to where I stood, and I felt a little relief when the much older one smiled at me. He had kind eyes, a mixture of brown and green and outlined with age, and even though I didn't know a single thing about him, I hoped this man was going to be my boss.

"Can we help you?" the other man spoke, and I looked over to him.

"I'm Josie. I'm supposed to meet with Jack Smelcer this morning for my first day."

"That would be me." He flicked his pen in the air, and I suddenly felt disappointed. "Give me just a minute."

I nodded and took a step back, but the other gentleman stuck his hand out in my direction.

I gripped his hand in mine just as he spoke. "I'm Mr. Clermont. It's nice to meet you, Josie."

Shit. This was Beck's dad. "It's nice to meet you too. I didn't mean to interrupt you all."

"You're not interrupting." He sounded so sincere. "I was actually looking forward to meeting you. Your father called me a few moments ago to let me know you'd be working with us."

I bit down on the inside of my bottom lip to stop myself from screaming. Of course he had. "I'm sorry. He shouldn't have bothered you."

He cocked his head to the side slightly, studying me with a warm smile on his face. "It's no bother. I'm glad I could be here to meet you when you arrived."

I shifted on my feet, nervous because I had no idea what I was supposed to say. I doubted it was customary for the owner to come out to meet the new server. The kings rarely came out to greet the help. "I appreciate it."

"Your father said he didn't want you to get a job, but you're stubborn."

"He has no room to talk." If my father screwed this up for me, I would be pissed. "I'm sorry. I shouldn't have said that."

"No." He chuckled as he shook his head. "He certainly doesn't. He also tried to talk me out of giving you this job."

I went stock-still because I knew what would happen next. If I hadn't already wanted to kill my father, I certainly did now.

"But I told him he could kick rocks."

I couldn't stop the small snort that left me. I doubt anyone typically talked to my father in that sort of way.

"So, I get to keep the job?" I asked hesitantly as I looked between them.

"Of course, you do. Your dad is an old friend, but he doesn't get to tell me who I can and can't hire."

I could have sworn there was a small shift in his eyes when he called my father a friend, but the people here didn't feel the same for my father as I did.

They worshipped him and used his friendship to their advantage.

"Thank you." I was sincere. My father held the power over everything in my life, and I didn't know what would happen if he was to use that power against me. My chest felt like it would collapse when I thought of him having my mother's house, but I would survive. It was just a house. Just things.

None of it really mattered.

Not when she was already gone.

"If you need anything, let me know." He patted my shoulder as he walked by me, and he smelled like old leather and warmth.

He smelled like a man who had worked very hard for the things he had.

"I will. Thank you."

I looked back to Jack, and he looked annoyed. He probably thought I was some spoiled little princess who needed her daddy to get me a job, and I hated that my father had given him that impression of me.

"This way." He nodded his head toward the kitchen, and I

followed him silently. We made our way into the serving area where everyone seemed to be waiting on him.

Jack started going over the chef specials for the day, reading them from a fancy menu in his hand, and I tried to memorize everything he was saying.

He pointed to the girl about my age who stood across from me with her long blonde hair in a ponytail. "This is Allie. Allie, this is Josie."

She smiled at me, and I smiled back even though I could feel everyone else's eyes on me.

"You'll be training with Allie this week. She's one of the best servers we have."

Allie smiled brighter, and if anyone else cared about what he said they didn't show it. Instead, they all looked bored and ready to get this small meeting over with.

I tried to pay attention as Jack droned on and on about the happenings of that day, but it was difficult. I was too busy trying to take in every detail about the people around me. They weren't exactly what I had expected.

They didn't seem like the pretentious assholes I thought they'd be.

Like the people at that party.

Well, except for Jack.

He finished talking, and I shifted on my feet. Allie waved at me with a smile that was the most genuine thing I'd seen since I arrived in this town. She leaned against the drink station as soon as Jack walked away. "Jack is kind of a douchebag."

I snorted out a laugh. "He always like that?" I looked over my shoulder to make sure he was long gone.

"Yeah. Or worse. Don't worry, the rest of us are cool."

She pulled two aprons off a shelf and handed me one. "Come on. Let me show you where to put your bag."

I followed behind her and listened as everyone said their

hellos. Allie was clearly liked, and I wondered how long she had worked here. She couldn't be much older than me.

"How long have you worked here?" I finally asked her as I helped her prep for lunch.

She handed me a knife, and I set it at the place setting like she had shown me.

"Since I was fifteen." She tucked a stray piece of hair behind her ear. "I work a lot more during the summer. Not so much once school starts. Clermont High isn't too bad though. I still have time to study and work." She laughed and I winced. "What?" She looked at me curiously.

"I'm going to Clermont Bay Prep."

"By choice?"

I couldn't help but laugh at the look on her face. "No. My dad is making me."

"I'm sorry." She seemed sincere, and that only served to jack up my anxiety about the school year. "It's not that bad."

I made a face showing just how little I believed her, and she laughed.

"There are a few cool people, but most of them are..." She looked like she was searching for the right word, so I helped her.

"Rich assholes?"

"Exactly." She snapped her fingers. "We already have to wait on them hand and foot here. I couldn't imagine having to go to school with them too."

"I'm not looking forward to it." I followed her as we carried the silverware to the next table. At least I would have Lucas. Even if I knew no one else there, I would have him.

"There are some really hot guys though." She fanned herself. "A lot of them are members here. You'll see."

All I could think about was Beck.

I followed her through the rest of the setup, and I couldn't stop the anxiety from rising as I thought about school. It was only a few weeks away, and I was supposed to be having the most fun year of my life. Instead, I would be spending my senior year with people who meant nothing to me.

With people who hated me for nothing.

Not that the people back home had meant much to me either. I had shut them all out once Mom got sick, and I barely knew any of them anymore.

And they certainly didn't know me.

Not the real me.

I barely knew who the real me was anymore.

I didn't know who I was without my mom.

I followed Allie's every move as patrons started rolling in. It was mostly men who were there to discuss business or who were there to talk shit while they golfed. They mostly talked business, sometimes about their wives, others about their mistresses. While I was shocked by it all, Allie seemed completely unfazed.

They talked as if we weren't even there. As if our presence was completely inconsequential, and I guess it was.

We were the people who didn't matter.

These men, they did.

And they knew it.

No one here would dare say a word. That was one of the advantages of Clermont Bay Country Club. Allie had made it clear that the secrets of these men lived and died within these walls.

There was no judgment, at least none that was voiced, and there were very few rules.

Secrecy was number one.

Break it and you were gone. Break it and you would never have the privilege these men shared again.

We were several hours into our shift when the sound of laughter caught my attention. I turned toward the entrance to watch a group of teenagers walk in. They were dressed far more casually than the rest of the members, but they still reeked of money.

"Who are they?" I whispered as Allie grabbed a fresh pitcher of water.

I watched them sit at the large table in the center of the room like they owned the place. They didn't care who sat around them or the type of power they possessed.

They feared nothing.

"Those, my dear, are your new schoolmates." I tensed as the words left her mouth. "The one in the corner, that's Carson Hale. He's a total playboy." Allie rolled her eyes, and her hands tightened around the pitcher. "He has a new girl on his arm every time you see him. I don't even know that girl's name that's with him today."

I could see why. He was handsome in a way that screamed money. His blond hair was perfectly coiffed but still somehow reminded me of a surfer. His shirt stark white and not a wrinkle in sight. His arrogance fueled by the idea that no one could touch him.

"The one sitting across from him, that's Olly Warner. His family is crazy rich. He's never going to have to work for anything. He's never worked for anything in his life."

I could barely see him from where I stood. He looked like a mess of light brown curls, and I imagined what they would feel like slipping through my fingers. He was fit, probably an athlete, and I found myself eager to get a look at his face.

Allie looked like she was eager to get as far away from them all as possible.

"Who's the girl sitting next to him?" She was gorgeous. Her body slender, her hair so dark it was almost black, and I couldn't help noticing how Olly watched her every move.

"That's Frankie Clermont." Allie practically growled out her name. "Her parents own this place."

"Oh." My gaze snapped back to Frankie, and I took in every

detail of her again. My heart raced as I watched her smile. She seemed so much kinder than her brother.

She didn't seem anything like him outside of the similarities in their looks.

Her tan skin and dark hair reminded me so much of Beck, but her smile, that belonged to her father.

"You don't like her?"

"It's not that." Allie shook her head. "They're all just so different than us."

I didn't tell her that my father was just as rich as them. Even if it was the truth, it didn't matter. That fact didn't make me anything like those people.

I looked back to the table just as he walked up. Beck grinned as he pulled out a seat next to his sister, and he looked so relaxed. I felt anything but.

My hands began sweating and my pulse crashed against my skin. I should have listened to Lucas. I never should have taken a job here.

"That one there." Allie grinned and fanned her face dramatically. "That's Beck Clermont."

My gaze swung to hers, and she giggled.

"Yeah," she answered before I could even voice my question. "He and Frankie are siblings. He's the heir to all of this."

She thought I was impressed by his last name. She thought that I cared about him at all.

I looked back to where he now sat, and my breath caught when my eyes met his. My stomach tightened as Allie placed one of the water pitchers in my hand.

"They all run this damn town."

I couldn't pull my gaze away from his long enough to even spare a glance at the rest of them. I had no idea who the others were, but it didn't matter. All that mattered was that he was here, and I had made a mistake.

She laughed before bumping into my shoulder. "You ready?"

I jerked my gaze back to her, and I tried to calm my racing heart. "I don't think I can do this."

Allie laughed, and I knew she probably thought I was being dramatic. These people were going to be my peers, and that was enough reason for me to fear going out there.

I didn't have to tell her that Beck hated me.

I didn't want to.

I didn't want to give voice to the fact that I cared about him at all.

"Come on."

I avoided his side of the table as I followed Allie's lead. She had a large smile on her face that didn't look one bit forced, but I knew I looked nothing like her. I chewed on my bottom lip as my hands shook around the pitcher.

"Good evening. Can we start you all off with some water?"

Someone grunted a noncommittal yes, but I didn't dare look to see who. I kept my head down, and I grabbed the first glass off the table.

"You must be new here. I don't think I've seen you before."

I looked up at the one who Allie told me was Olly, and I was right. He was just as good-looking from the front as he was from the back. Especially when he was smiling at me like that.

"I am." I nodded but didn't volunteer any other information. I didn't care if that made me rude. I didn't need these people knowing anything about me.

I was sure Beck would tell them everything they needed to know. He would tell them everything he thought he knew about me.

"You look familiar though." This time it was Frankie talking, and when I looked at her, I could have sworn there was something about her that didn't make her anything like these other people. "What's your name?"

"Josie." I cleared my throat as I grabbed the next glass, and I stupidly let my gaze snap to Beck for only a moment. He was still staring at me, and he looked so damn angry.

He was motionless and eerily calm, and I hated that I felt like I was waiting for him to explode.

He was a bomb, and I would be the one to feel the effects of him. I would be the one he destroyed.

"Josie what?"

I didn't want to tell her my last name.

"Josie Vos." Beck's voice was soft and rich as my name rolled from his lips, and I thought I was going to break the glass as I tried to calm my shaking hand around it.

The table was harshly quiet for a moment, and I knew that whatever Beck's reason was for hating me was widely known among the rest of them.

"You're Lucas Vos's sister?" This time it was the girl with Carson that spoke.

I hated how she said his name. "Stepsister."

"Holy shit."

I had no idea who said that. I placed the glass back down on the table with a still trembling hand and grabbed another. The sooner I could get away from this table, the better. I could feel them all staring at me, even Allie, but it was him who finally made me look up again.

He was staring at me again, and I watched his Adam's apple bob.

He picked up his glass, and I watched as he brought it to his full lips. Lips I had tasted before I knew who he was. It felt like everyone in the entire room was watching him, but he was still watching me.

He took a long drag from his glass, and his eyes didn't leave mine as I watched the glass slip through his fingers. The loud crash of breaking glass pulled me out of whatever trance he seemed to put me in, and I rushed to Allie's side as she bent to clean up the mess.

"Allie, I'd love another water."

Allie stopped with a large piece of glass in her hand and stared at me as he spoke. Her eyes were round in shock, and I knew that she felt as confused as I did.

"Okay. Let me get this cleaned up, and I'll get it right to you."

He turned in his chair, looking down at us with pure venom in his voice. "I think the new girl can handle it."

I could tell that Allie had no idea what to do. She looked from him to me, and I gave her a slight nod of my head. As much as I didn't want to be left alone with him, there was no way that I would subject her to whatever he was going to do next. She hesitated before she stood, and I knew that she didn't want to leave me here alone.

I collected the glass in my hand as fast as I could, eager to get away from him. I barely felt it as the glass slid into my skin. I tightened my hand around it, letting the burn of the cut ricochet through me. It took everything inside me not to tell all of them to go straight to hell, but I needed this job. I needed it far more than I needed any of them to like me.

"You're bleeding." His voice held no concern.

"I'm fine."

"I wasn't worried about you."

I finally looked back up at him then.

"Don't drop an ounce of that Vos blood on my carpet."

"Beck." It was his sister who spoke, but he shrugged her off as if she was nothing.

Instead, he leaned closer to me, his face almost level with mine as he spoke. "I don't want to see any Vos blood unless it's at my hands."

I shot back as his words hit me like a whip. He wanted to draw blood from my family? From me?

"I am only a Vos by blood." I barely knew anything about this guy other than his last name, but he thought he knew everything about me simply by mine.

He reached out. His hand landed on my cheek gently, and I hated that I flinched at his touch. "You're still one of them." He ran his thumb against my bottom lip, and my thighs tightened involuntarily.

He touched me as if he somehow had the right, and I wanted to snap his fingers in half.

"Fuck you." I heard the others get eerily quiet at my words, but I didn't care. I needed this job, but not that damn bad. If he wanted to fire me, then he could go ahead and do so, but I would be damned if I sat there and listened to him.

I rose to my feet, his broken glass in my hands, and I hated how intrigued he looked. He cocked his head to the side, and it was as if I was the only thing he could see. His focus was singular, and it was completely on me.

My teeth felt like they were going to crack as I stared at him. His eyes looked so dark they were almost black, and I couldn't look away. Even though he had a small grin on his face that showed his perfect teeth, it was as if his eyes were dead.

"Don't let me see you here again." His words sounded sweet coming off his tongue, but I could still see the venom in his eyes.

"Or what?" I didn't know why I said it. I felt eager to push him. He made me eager to find out what he was capable of.

He and I were complete strangers, but somehow, he felt like anything but. He apparently knew far more about me than I knew of him, and I hated that he had that advantage. But even through his palpable hatred, there was something about him that still made my heart race in more than fear.

He stood. His height towering over me, and I lifted my chin as I stared into his eyes. "Don't test me, Vos."

I had a feeling he wasn't used to being tested. I had a feeling nobody ever questioned him.

It was time that changed.

"Then fire me, Clermont." I took a step closer to him, and the smell of his cologne overwhelmed me. It reminded me of that moment on the beach. Before we became more than two strangers. Before everything was ruined. "If you have that power."

He tensed, his body going stone-still. My hands throbbed around the glass, and I could feel my pulse booming through every part of me.

"If not, I need to get back to work." I stepped to the side with every intention of passing him, then avoiding this table for the rest of the night, but his hand reached out and gripped my upper arm before I could escape him.

His skin felt like it was a flame against mine.

His face was so close to me and my stomach tightened against my better judgment. My head and body as much at war as I appeared to be with him.

"If you don't leave." He licked his bottom lip, and I couldn't stop myself from tracking the slow movement. "I'll make your life a living hell."

CHAPTER FOUR

I had no fucking clue what she was doing here.

Was her father insane?

What the hell did he think was going to happen? He sent his daughter straight into my hands, and he thought that she would make it out unscathed?

"Did you know that someone hired Lucas Vos's sister?" I stormed into my father's office as my muscles shook. I didn't care that he was on the phone. I didn't care that his gaze snapped up to me and he looked as annoyed with me as I was with him.

"I'll call you back in a bit." He set his phone down on his desk with more force than necessary and looked at me. "Yes. I knew. Joseph called me this morning."

I had to bite my tongue to not rage out at him. My teeth felt like they might snap from the pressure of keeping it all together. The fact that he still spoke to that man made my skin crawl. How the two of them could pretend like nothing had ever happened was despicable.

"Fire her." I dug my fingers into the back of the leather chair that sat across from him and tried to rein in my temper.

He shook his head, and my fingers turned white under the force of my hold. "I'm not firing the girl because you don't like her brother." His tone was final, brooking no room for argument.

My head snapped back. "Do you remember what her brother did?" I spit at him.

His eyes snapped up to mine at my words, and I knew that I was walking a fine line. My dad was kind and humble, but he refused to deal with disrespect. It was the thing that drove me the craziest about this whole situation.

It was as if they were rubbing their disrespect right in his face.

"I haven't forgotten." He leaned forward, his nostrils flaring, and clasped his hands together. "I will never forget what that boy did. But she is not him."

I had never seen my father as weak. Not until recently. Not until I saw the way he handled this.

But he felt weak now.

It was like I didn't know him at all.

"Joseph said she has agreed to be on her best behavior, but she wants a job. He feels more comfortable about her working here than someplace he can't control."

"But he has all the control here, doesn't he?" The tightness in my chest intensified as I snapped at my father.

"Watch your tone, Beckham." My dad rose, and I hated the way he had to grip the desk to pull himself to his full height. I hated watching him wither away.

"I'm sorry." I was sincere. I didn't want to talk to my dad like this, but the thought of her being here was driving me mad. The thought of Frankie having to put up with it made me tremble with rage. "But you can't expect me to work with her. You can't expect me to just forget."

"No one is asking you to forget." He ran his hand over his hair that was identical to mine, except for the dusting of gray at his temples. "But you are going to have to learn to work with people you don't want to."

I opened my mouth to tell him this was different, but he didn't allow me a moment to speak.

"You're going to be getting all of this." He held his arms out, but I knew he meant more than this place. "And you're going to be getting it earlier than any of us expected."

"We don't know that, Dad." I shook my head and my chest suddenly felt like it was caving in. He was telling the truth regardless of whether I wanted to hear it. He always had, whether it hurt me or not. The man would always be honest with me.

"I hate Joseph Vos."

I looked up at him, shocked by his admission. The way they had worked together, the way they had swept everything under the rug like it didn't fucking happen, made me think the exact opposite.

"I hate him, I hate his vile fucking son, and I hate that it is necessary for me to continue to work with him. But Joseph Vos is important. He invests in this place." He pointed down to his desk. "He invests in this town. And we are far too smart to burn a bridge that we still might need to cross. If I hadn't worked with him, your ass wouldn't be here right now."

I knew he was right. I knew that he did what he had to do to protect me, but it still made me feel like I was burning from the inside out.

"This girl has nothing to do with what Lucas did. She had no part in it."

He was wrong though. She was one of them, and she would pay for the sins of her family. She would be the exact piece I needed to pay her brother back for every fucking vile thing he did.

I didn't care what anyone else said. I didn't care that my father wanted that bridge to stay intact. I would burn it to the fucking ground.

And I didn't care if she got hurt along the way.

I hoped she did.

She was one of them, and no matter how innocent my father said she was, she couldn't have come from a man like Joseph Vos and be completely sinless.

I just had to figure out her weaknesses, then I would use them to bring the Vos family to the ground.

CHAPTER FIVE

JOSIE

"You are going to a party with me this weekend." Allie picked up another fork and wiped away the watermarks with a rag.

We were two of the only staff left after a slow Wednesday night, and it felt odd to be here without the normal hustle and bustle.

Allie had her feet up on one of the chairs, and there was a pile of silverware between us.

"There's no way that's going to happen. I told you what happened at the last party I went to." I had. After she saw the way Beck had treated me in the country club, I had vented to her about the entire thing.

For a moment, it bothered me that she was so shocked by what I was saying. She had never seen Beck act like this before. She had told me that Beck had always been kind, even if he was always untouchable.

But I couldn't fathom thinking of Beck as kind. He had been the farthest thing from kind that I had ever met.

Except for those few moments before I knew the real him.

"This party won't be like that." She dropped a clean fork in the bin and grabbed another. "This is a Clermont High party. None of those Prep boys ever show up."

"Really?" Even as she said it, I knew it still probably wasn't a good idea.

"Yeah. Even your brother doesn't show his face around there." She cut her hand through the air. "They draw the line in the sand of who they think is important or not. It's all about money."

I winced. Even though I didn't touch my father's money, I was still benefiting from it. I was living in his large home and driving one of his extra cars. I never worried about bills or meals, and I felt guilty for it.

Even though that was insane, I couldn't shake it.

"So, it'll be safe?"

"Yes." She dropped her feet and turned toward me with a smile on her face. "Plus, there are some guys who I go to school with that I could introduce you to."

I laughed, but my stomach tightened as I thought about Beck. "I don't think having a guy should be anywhere on my radar right now."

"You don't have to date them." She rolled her eyes, and I swear mine practically bugged out. "It's called friends with benefits, Josie."

I didn't want to tell her that I was very limited on experience where benefits were involved. I was seventeen years old, and most girls my age were far more experienced than me.

I wasn't ashamed of the fact, but I would be lying if I said it didn't make me feel the slightest bit embarrassed and behind.

My only sexual experience had been awkward and unpleasurable, consisting of a boy's hand down my pants who had no idea what he was doing.

I threw my towel at Allie's head as my cheeks reddened. "I am not getting a friend with benefits."

"Why not?" She laughed, and the way she smiled made it feel like the idea was the simplest thing to her. "You holding out for a hate fuck from Beck?"

My mouth dropped open, and she threw her head back in laughter. "I was just kidding." She held up her hands. "Unless you are?"

I shook my head quickly, but I swear my stomach felt like there was a rubber band being pulled tightly inside it. I felt like it may snap at any moment.

"Oh my God. Are you a virgin?"

"Shh." I leaned forward and slammed my hand down on her mouth.

"You are." Her words were muffled around my hand, and her eyes bulged out of her face.

"Would you shut up?"

"No one else is here." She waved around us, and I let go of her mouth. "The guys in the kitchen can't hear a thing we say."

I sat back down in my seat and grabbed a spoon. I stared down at the silver as I rubbed and rubbed with the towel in my hand.

"I didn't mean to embarrass you. I'm just shocked." Allie's voice was so sincere, and I dropped the spoon in the bin before looking back up at her.

"I'm not embarrassed." I totally was.

"You're hot." Allie laughed. "The boys in this town are going to be fighting over you before the school year even starts."

I knew she was just trying to distract me from being embarrassed, but I still appreciated her compliment.

"I think I just need to stay away from all the boys in this town." I laughed. "Apparently, they don't like me."

Allie grinned just as we heard a loud crash from the hallway before laughter rang out. Allie straightened her shirt as she stood, and I followed suit. It was probably one of the guys from the kitchen, but I didn't want Jack to catch us sprawled out at one of the tables gabbing about boys.

"Shit."

I looked around Allie just as Carson pushed through the door. He stumbled slightly, and it was clear that he was drunk.

"What are you doing here?" Allie's voice was strained as she took the smallest step back.

"Allie!" He practically cheered her name just as Olly and Beck walked in behind him.

I held my breath as I watched him swagger into the room. He was grinning as his eyes met mine, and I knew he had to be intoxicated because the smile didn't fall from his face.

"Well, looky here." He pulled out a chair and sat down with his feet wide and his arms loose. He would look so at ease if it wasn't for the way his jaw tightened.

I knew better than to trust any sort of calmness from him.

It almost scared me more. The way Beck was looking at me felt like the calm before the storm, and I didn't want to get caught in his onslaught.

"We didn't realize you guys were here." Allie sounded so professional. "We'll get out of your way."

She reached for my hand, but Beck's voice stopped us both.

"Stay." He cocked his head just slightly, and I could feel him staring at me. "I already warned Josie once to not be here, but she didn't listen." My spine straightened and the urge to run from the room was overwhelming. "So stay. Finish your work."

Allie turned to me, but I was still looking at him. I felt like he was a snake and I was his prey, and if I dared look away for even a second he would strike. If I dared to turn away from him, he would make me realize my mistake.

Allie moved back to the table, and the two of us started working again silently. Carson had a bottle of liquor in his hands, and he chugged from it before passing it to one of the others.

I wasn't sure if this was normal behavior for them, but the way Allie sat with her back perfectly straight and her eyes constantly darting to them made me think it wasn't.

The three of them laughed and talked as Allie and I finished up what we were doing, and it felt like it had been hours since they walked in the room. I knew it had only been minutes, but every second felt excruciatingly long as I watched him.

I had no idea what they were thinking, what their plan was tonight as they looked like they didn't give a shit, but I knew that I didn't trust a single one of them.

I stood with Allie and the two of us carried the bins of silverware over to the bar.

"Josie." Beck's voice was smooth and effortless, and my stomach fluttered at the sound. "Come here."

Allie looked up at me, and I knew that she was willing to

tell him to go to hell if I wanted her to, but part of me wanted to know what he wanted.

I wanted to end whatever game he was playing and just get it the hell over with.

I walked toward him, but every part of my body warned me to stop. My breathing was rushed, my hands shook, and I felt like every part of me knew that I should fear him.

"What?" I stopped several feet away from him and linked my fingers together in front of me.

"A little closer." He crooked his finger as he bit down on his lip, and it was as if every bit of anger he had shown me before was replaced with lust.

He was looking at me like he wanted to devour me. He was looking at me like he had on the beach, but there were no pretenses of him being a nice guy.

This Beck felt like pure sin, and I was an idiot as I stepped closer until I was just out of his reach.

He leaned forward in his chair, his elbows resting on his knees, and his gaze raked over every inch of my body. His scrutiny of me felt tangible and forbidden. He hadn't even touched me, and my entire body felt tight with need.

Need to get away from him.

Need to be closer.

"What do you want, Beck?" I hated the way he was making me feel. I felt like a whirlwind of confusion when it came to him, and I would rather just deal with his hate.

With his hate, I knew exactly where I stood.

I knew what to expect.

"I want a lot of things, Josie." He rubbed his chin as he spoke, and I noticed that Carson and Olly were both watching us.

They were waiting for a show.

"I need to get back to work." It was a lie. We were finished for the night, and the only thing I needed to do was clock out before I ran out of this place without looking back.

Allie was still standing next to the bar, and I knew that she wouldn't leave without me.

"What you need is to get on your fucking knees."

I took a sharp inhale of breath as my gaze slammed into his.

"I've been thinking about that pretty little mouth of yours." His eyes were so dark, and I didn't know how much of this was really him and how much was the alcohol. "I can't wait to see what your lips look like stretched around my cock."

My gaze darted to Olly who was leaned back in his chair with a small smile on his face. They weren't affected at all by what their friend was saying.

"Don't look at him." Beck's voice held all the venom that I had become used to, and I didn't hesitate to follow his command. I looked away from Olly and shifted on my feet as I looked back at Beck.

I should have told him to shut up. I should have slapped the shit out of him and walked away, but I did neither of those things. I stared into his eyes that felt like they were going to consume me, and I tried my hardest not to squeeze my thighs together as an ache began to build there.

"You only look at me." He was so fucking sure of himself, so sure of what he was capable of. "When I fuck that mouth of yours, you only look at me."

"That's never going to happen." My voice was sure, but I felt rattled to my core.

"Don't challenge me, doll." He grinned, and I had a feeling that even though it rarely happened, Beck loved being challenged. "You won't like how it ends."

"It's not a challenge." I was acting far braver than I felt. "It's a promise. You will never touch me."

His smile became almost sinister, and I could barely catch my breath. "God, this is going to be fun." He stood from his chair, and I thought he was going to touch me now. My body froze and the only thing I could hear was my heart racing.

I had known Beck was an ass. He proved that to me the day I met him, but I hadn't actually feared him until this moment.

I feared what he was going to do.

I feared how far he would take his hate for Lucas.

I feared *him*.

He lifted the bottle from the table and tipped it forward. The brown liquor hit the table in a cascade and trickled down the sides before hitting the floor.

Beck held my gaze the entire time. He didn't care what kind of mess he made. He didn't give two shits about the things he ruined.

He was just fucking things up without a single thought of the repercussions.

"If you won't get on your knees for me..." He lifted the bottle, making sure every last drop fell from the lip before dropping it on the table with a loud smack. He took a step closer to me, and I held my ground and didn't move away from him, even though every single part of me wanted to retreat.

He reached his hand out and ran his thumb over my bottom lip as he stared at my mouth. I felt frozen under his touch, the soft caress a complete contrast to the way he was looking at me. "Then get on your knees and clean up this fucking mess."

CHAPTER
SIX

"Beck, pick up your shoes." Frankie kicked one of my sneakers out of her way as she dropped down on the couch across from me with a huff. "You're such a pig."

I rolled my eyes and lowered the volume on the baseball game that had been providing me with a distraction, with the hope of silencing my racing mind. "But you still love me."

"Not today." She shot me her beautiful smile, and it made my chest tighten. Just that one small smile felt like such a different Frankie.

It felt like the old Frankie.

"Liar." I winked at my baby sister.

"So, are we going to discuss her?" Frankie's voice grew quiet, and I immediately knew who she was referring to. Josie.

We hadn't discussed the incident at the country club when her identity was revealed to Frankie and the guys. I had silenced my friends as soon as they even tried mentioning her, and as expected, it wasn't a topic of conversation Frankie wanted to divulge in; until now.

"Not much to discuss." I felt her eyes on me, and reluctantly, I looked away from the television and over to her. "Honestly, Frankie. She's no one."

"But she is someone." Her voice came out soft, and I hated that this conversation was taking her back to the worst time of her life. Fuck the Voses. Fuck. Them.

I gritted my teeth. My need to protect my sister and to get revenge for everything she'd been through came pouring out of me.

"Yeah. Someone who will stay the fuck away from us. Especially you."

She nodded, her slight smile this time not reaching her eyes. "Okay, Beck."

"I love when you agree with me so easily."

"And just like that, cocky Beck shows his face."

"Did he ever leave?"

"You're such an idiot."

"Not the worst thing I've been called."

"Oh my God. Stop." She rolled her eyes.

"What are you two arguing about now?" My mom plopped down on the sofa next to me, and I immediately reached out and stole some popcorn from her bowl. She slapped at my hand, but I didn't let it stop me.

"Him being ridiculously cocky and not cleaning up after himself." Frankie reached forward, and my mom held the bowl out for her.

"That's because he's spoiled." She patted my cheek playfully as she grinned. It's the curse of the firstborn. "That's why you're my favorite, Frankie."

"Hey." I was actually insulted.

She laughed as she ran her fingers through my hair and moved it out of my face. She was constantly begging me to get a haircut, and I was constantly telling her that my hair was fine.

My mother had always been overprotective and a little over-bearing, but she had always put Frankie and me before anything else.

"You are both my favorite children. Don't worry."

Frankie stuck her tongue out at me because while I had been a mama's boy almost my entire life, she had been Mom's baby since the moment she came into this world.

"Where's Dad?"

"He went to bed early." My mom's smile was sad, and I knew it was because my father wasn't feeling well. There were far too many nights when he wasn't feeling well.

"I'm probably going to hit the hay soon too. I've got work-outs tomorrow." I stretched and patted my stomach.

"Are you ready for baseball to start back up?"

I had been playing since I was old enough to remember. It was something that I loved forever, and it had always loved me back. It had been my constant through every other change in my life.

And it was something I would no longer be playing after this year.

So I was ready for it to start back up, but it felt bittersweet. "I am. I'm getting out of shape."

Frankie rolled her eyes, and my mom laughed.

"You make me sick, Beckham."

"I can't help it that I'm the one who got Mom's good genes." I didn't look a thing like my mother except for my smile. Every other part of me was a spitting image of my dad.

But my mom still grinned at my comment.

"Go to bed so Mom and I can bond and turn on a chick flick."

I laughed and stood from the couch. "I'm going." I leaned down and kissed my mom on her cheek. "I love you."

"I love you."

I tugged on Frankie's ponytail as I passed behind her. "I love you too, dork."

"Love you." She sounded so annoyed, but I knew the truth.

She loved me as much as I loved her, and I regretted how I used to never tell her. I wouldn't make a mistake like that again.

And like she had so many fucking times since I met her, Josie flashed through my head. I wondered if Lucas told her he loved her. Did they sit together at their house and pretend like they were something like a loving family? And more than anything, I wondered if she had any clue at the astronomically huge asshole she was living with. She couldn't be that naïve, could she?

I opened my phone as I laid down in my bed, and I let my finger hover over her name. I should have probably been ashamed that I had taken her phone number from the files at work, but I wasn't.

I had no room for shame.

I had contemplated texting her since the moment I got it. It was the reason Olly, Carson, and I had been at the country club so late the other night. I didn't realize she would still be there. That was just the icing on the cake.

The way she had watched me as I spoke to her. The way her mouth parted involuntarily as my thumb moved across her soft lip.

I wasn't lying to her when I said I had imagined her pretty mouth wrapped around my cock. I had imagined it over and over as I leaned against the shower wall and jacked off to the thought of her.

I hated her, but I desperately wanted to fuck her.

I wanted to take the edge off my rage by pounding into her mouth or that tight little body of hers.

Just seeing her reaction to me the other night had made me hard as a rock. She may have hated me as much as I hated her, but the way her body hummed with anticipation wasn't from hate.

She wanted me too.

I typed Cami's name and clicked on it before I did something stupid. I could just text Cami right now and get the release that I needed. I could use her the same way we had been using each other for years, but I couldn't bring myself to type out the message.

Cami wasn't what I wanted.

Just the thought of texting her felt like a chore.

I quickly hit Cancel and pulled Josie's name back up. I quickly hit Send on the message before I could change my mind.

I can't stop thinking about you on your knees.

I watched as the message went from delivered to read, but there was no response. I wasn't surprised.

I tucked my arm under my head as I stared at my phone.

Have you thought about it too?

The three little dots danced across my screen before they disappeared. She was reading my messages and thinking about what to say. Even if she hadn't said a word, that thought alone made my dick strain against my shorts.

What you would look like with my hands in your hair as I fucked your mouth?

I pulled my cock out of my shorts and rested my hand against it.

I want to know what you would taste like after I came in your mouth. I wonder if I could still taste the sweetness of you beneath the taste of me.

It was only a second later before her text chimed on my phone.

Stop.

But I wouldn't stop.

God. You would be so wet.

I pushed the bead of precum over the head of my cock as I thought about it. Josie tried to act like she was innocent, but I could just imagine how turned on she'd be.

Her lips would be swollen from me and her pussy would be begging me even if she was too stubborn to.

Are you wet right now?

I imagined she was. Her small hands were probably shaking as she timidly slid them into her panties and felt her own arousal against her fingers.

I wondered if that would shock her or if she already knew how badly she wanted me.

Move that wetness around. Smear it over your clit and imagine it was me.

There was a long moment with no answer, and my cock felt like it was going to explode in my hand.

Are you doing it?

Are you imagining it was me?

Beck, stop.

God. It was like I could hear her whispering my name.

Whatever you're doing right now, I would do it better. I would be rougher.

I wouldn't stop even when you begged me.

My breathing was coming out in harsh bursts, and I imagined my hand was hers.

I was so fucking close.

Why are you doing this?

Why? Why? She knew why. She knew exactly how I felt about her and her fucking family.

Because I want you to beg for it.

A bolt of pleasure shot through my lower back and into my thighs.

I want to hear you beg me for everything I give you.

I won't.

Her response was immediate, and it was a dare.

She would beg me, and then I would make her regret it.

She would regret ever coming to Clermont Bay.

You will.

Pleasure crashed through me, and I came all over my fingers and on my stomach in a rush. I could barely control myself as I came to the thought of her.

CHAPTER
SEVEN

JOSIE

I had no idea how I let her talk me into this.

I had no business going to a party, but Allie had assured me that this would be different.

It would be different than the last party I attended and different from every other time I had any interaction with Beck.

Allie and I had both worked a long shift, and I just wanted to relax. I didn't want to think about Beck, his hate, or the way I couldn't stop thinking about the text messages he had sent me the other night.

I wasn't even sure how he had gotten my number, but I didn't have time to worry about that. I was far too concerned over his filthy mouth and how I had done exactly like he told me and slid my fingers into my panties as I read his words on my phone.

Shame prickled every part of my skin, but it hadn't stopped me.

No one was there, and Beck had no idea what I was doing. He probably thought that I was angered by his texts, and I was. I was angry and hot and frustrated.

And his words washed over me as if he had never been anyone except the guy I first met. I imagined what it would be like if Beck didn't hate me, and I let myself pretend my hand was his.

Every time I had told him to stop, I was begging him for more in my mind, and it hadn't taken long.

I came so quickly as I imagined his hand, and the shame I had been pushing away was the only thing I had left to feel.

He was cruel and brazen, and I shouldn't have been turned on by anything he did or said.

Allie threw me my bag, and we both changed clothes in the front seats of her Honda. I chucked my black dress pants and dress shirt in the back seat and slipped on a pair of ripped jean shorts and a simple white t-shirt. Allie looked far dressier than

I did in a short yellow sundress that made her look absolutely incredible.

I fluffed my long brown hair in the sun visor mirror and tried to calm my nerves as she slid lip gloss over her lips. Tonight wasn't about Beck or what he wanted or didn't want. Tonight was about having fun. Something I hadn't done in a really long time.

"It'll mostly be Clermont High students here." She nodded out toward the beach as she dropped her lip gloss in the cupholder. "Prep students are usually all off vacationing for the summer."

I chuckled and twisted my mom's ring on my finger. I hated feeling so out of my element.

Although I didn't even know what my element was anymore. I didn't know where the hell I belonged.

We walked into the sand, me a step behind Allie, both of us in search of the light of the bonfire. There were dozens of people standing around the fire, some of them in bathing suits as if they had spent the entire day on the beach. Others looking like they had spent the entire day drinking.

But this party already felt so vastly different from the last one I attended.

While it was still a bunch of teenagers who had no sense of responsibility or self-preservation, this party was much more laid back.

It was just them, the beach, and a tall keg full of beer.

Allie reached back for me, gripping my hand in hers just as we reached the crowd.

"Hey, Allie."

Allie waved at some girl and kept pulling me forward.

I didn't dare let go of her hand as we walked together. I barely knew Allie, but I knew that she was the closest thing to a friend I had.

Honestly, it felt like it had been forever since I had a real friend.

Not since my mom died.

It was my fault too. I had shut my friends out when my mom got sick. I couldn't stand their pity or the way their parents looked at me when I was around. Like I was some charity case because my mom had cancer.

It was how the whole school had looked at me. Most of them had gone to school with me for as long as I could remember, but suddenly I became different. I could see it all over their faces. I heard it in their whispers, and as much as I hated being in Clermont Bay, I was glad that I was no longer there. Especially without her.

"This is Josie."

I looked up at the guy she was talking to. He grinned at me as he pushed his floppy light brown hair out of his face.

He reached his hand out to me, and I couldn't help but stare at his abs that were clearly on display. He wore nothing but a pair of boardshorts and based on the deep tan of his skin, I'd bet anything that he spent the majority of his days on this beach.

"It's nice to meet you, Josie. I'm Will." He gripped my hand in his, his skin as warm as the setting sun, and I tried to think of a coherent thing to say back to him. My own skin warmed as I stared at him.

"You too."

He grinned, and I had a feeling that look rarely left his face.

"You new here?" I watched as his eyes looked me over subtly, but I noticed. Allie did too. She tried to hide her smile as she dropped my other hand.

"I'm going to go grab us a drink." She walked away from me, and I almost reached back out to stop her. I wasn't good at this.

This small talk with people I didn't know.

I looked back to Will with my stomach fluttering and finally answered his question. "Yeah. I just moved here." I could have told him more. He probably knew who my dad and my new step-brother were just like everyone else, but I didn't want him to know.

I didn't want him to treat me differently when I could do nothing to change it.

I didn't want him to treat me like Beck had.

"What do you think so far?" He took a step closer to me, away from his friends at his side.

"It's okay."

"Okay?" He chuckled. "Allie must be a terrible tour guide."

"She's not too bad."

"I don't know about that." He nodded out toward the ocean, and there was a sense of awe that smoothed out his features. "Do you have this kind of view where you come from?"

I followed his gaze and took in the sun dipping just below the farthest edge of the water. It seemed so impossibly beauti-ful. I hadn't even paid attention to it once since we got here.

"No." I shook my head. "Nothing like that."

"You been swimming yet?"

I looked over at Will, who seemed even closer than he was before. "No."

He reached out for my hand, his fingertips barely touching mine as he turned his back to the water. "Come on. Let's dip our toes in."

I knew this was nothing like when I had been on the beach with Beck, but I still hesitated. My heart raced as I looked over my shoulder for Allie, but she was talking to a group of girls who looked like they probably went to school with her. "I don't know."

"It's just your toes." I looked back at him as he spoke, and there was something about his smile that calmed me just the smallest bit. "What are you scared of?"

He was teasing and I knew it, but I hated what he said. I

wasn't scared. I refused to be. The girl I left back in Utah was scared.

Not me.

I took a step toward him, my fingers hanging loosely against his, and a dimple popped out on his cheek.

He led us to the edge of the water, and I kicked my shoes off in the sand. The water was cool as it lapped at my toes, and I tried to remember the last time I had touched the ocean.

Not just the damp sand or the spray of its waves.

Truly just jumped in.

It had to be close to five or six years ago. Before my mother had gotten sick.

"Is that really as far as you're going to go?" He trudged into the water without an ounce of fear, and I watched as the waves splashed against his legs.

I took another small step, and he laughed.

"You're a risk taker, aren't you?"

"You could tell that already?" I pushed my toes into the sand, then watched it disappear with the push and pull of the water.

"From the moment I saw you." He smiled and moved farther into the water. He beckoned me in, but there was no way I was getting in the water with him.

I had just gotten here, and I didn't know this guy.

It didn't matter that his smile put me at ease or that the look in his eyes dared me to do something more. I had learned my lesson about trusting boys in Clermont Bay. The first time was a mistake I wouldn't soon forget.

I shook my head just as he reached into the water and splashed me playfully.

"No." I held up my hands, as if that would somehow help me, and laughed.

It felt odd. I hadn't laughed in a long time. Not like this. Not so freely.

"Get in or it's happening." He was teasing me, but I didn't want to risk it.

I took off back toward the beach, but Will wrapped his arms around my waist and spun me back toward the water.

"No." I was laughing as he dropped me into the ocean, the water only hitting my knees. My stomach flipped, and my breathing was coming out in bursts.

"I warned you. You can't move to Clermont Bay and not experience the ocean. It's a sin, really."

"I'm experiencing it." I held my arms out to the sides and looked around. "Isn't this enough?"

"No." I wondered if Will looked at everyone the way he was looking at me.

If he had the power to make every girl feel special as soon as he met them.

He reached for me again, and I let him. I didn't know a single thing about this boy, but something about him made me feel like I could trust him. I knew how stupid that sounded. I was in the ocean with a guy I had never met, surrounded by more people that I didn't know, and I felt safe with him.

I felt like this moment, smiling with this boy, could somehow make me forget Beck.

I could forget the way he made me feel and the way I had given in to him without him even knowing.

Will lifted me over his shoulder and acted like he was going to jump into the water.

"No!" I screamed and laughed, and I heard others laughing from the beach.

"You sure?" he asked and I pushed against his back to raise my head.

"Yes. I've seen enough of the ocean. There are sharks in there."

He gently set me back down on my feet, my blood rushing

away from my head, and I knew that I still had a stupid smile on my face.

"There." He was right in front of me, and he pushed some of my hair out of my face. "There's the smile I wanted to see."

"I was smiling at you earlier." I laughed because there was a good possibility that he was insane.

"Yeah, but that one was fake."

I couldn't stop smiling because he was right. My thighs were covered in saltwater and sand, and small splatters of water dotted my clothes. I hadn't felt this carefree in a long time, too long to remember, but it felt good.

It didn't feel forced at all.

I wrapped my arms around his shoulders as a wave crashed into my calves, threatening to knock me over, and I could have sworn he smelled like the sun. He smelled like that moment when you had been out on the water all day and your skin still felt the heat of the sun. When you were tired but perfectly content.

His hair tickled my face as I breathed him in, and for a moment, I forgot. Where I was. Who I was. What I was supposed to be. I just forgot it all and let him hold on to me as he laughed around the sound of the ocean.

Then I looked up, and I saw him.

I didn't know where he had come from. But Beck stood next to the fire with his hands in his pockets and his callous eyes on me. Had he been here all along and I just missed him?

There was no way.

I would have noticed him. He was impossible to miss.

And it was clear that he hadn't missed me.

He didn't hide the fact that he was staring at me, even when my gaze met his, he didn't look away. He held my gaze, his anger hitting me as harshly as the waves, and I suddenly felt foolish in Will's arms.

And the fact that he made me feel that way heated my blood far more than Will's warmth ever could.

Beck Clermont hated me, that much was perfectly clear, and I didn't give two shits why. I hated him too.

He had forced me to hate him, and he was successful.

He looked like a king standing there. All the people on the beach vying for his attention, but he didn't move his gaze away from me. Not for one second.

I pushed away from Will, steadying myself on my feet, and I pulled my own gaze away from Beck long enough to look up at him.

"You okay?" He was still smiling, and it was so carefree and easy. It was the kind of smile that made you fall for someone. The kind of smile I should fall for.

But I couldn't help looking back over his shoulder at Beck.

"Yeah. I'm fine." I ran my fingers over my shorts, but Will was already looking back to where my attention kept wandering. He looked back to me, his smile faltering slightly, but I noticed.

He reached his hand out for me, and I let him pull me toward him and to the dry sand. "Let's go get you a drink." He put his arm over my shoulders as we walked, and I let him. He was a complete stranger, but I somehow felt safer there under his arm when I had no idea what faced me.

I avoided looking back toward Beck as we made our way over to a giant trash can that was stuck down in the sand. A keg was floating in ice, and Will let go of me as he started pouring me a cup. I didn't dare tell him that I didn't like beer. Instead, I gripped the plastic cup in my hand with too much force and I took a deep drink of the bitter liquid.

"It's cheap-ass beer." He chuckled when he saw my face. "But it does the trick."

I nodded and wiped the edge of my mouth with the back of

my hand. I didn't really know the difference between cheap beer and expensive beer, but I knew it tasted awful.

Will was looking back toward the fire, but I was looking anywhere else. "You know Beck Clermont?"

I tensed as the name left his mouth. "Not really. Why?" It wasn't a lie. I didn't know anything about him. Not in any way that actually mattered.

"He's staring at me like he wants to rip my head off." Will chuckled and looked down at me.

I chanced a look over my shoulder, and he was right. Beck was staring Will down as if he hated him as much as he hated me. Maybe he did.

Maybe he hated everyone.

But according to Allie, that wasn't true.

According to her, she had never seen him act toward anyone the way he did me.

Lucky me, I guess.

"Did you do something to piss him off?" I asked Will, even though I knew that hatred was probably directed at me.

"Not that I'm aware of." He chuckled again and pushed his hair out of his face. "I hope not at least."

"How do you know Beck?"

"Everyone knows Beck." Will looked at me like I was crazy. "He's the best player on the Prep baseball team. He's been offered a dozen college scholarships even though he doesn't need any of them." There was a hint of irritation or maybe jealousy in Will's voice, and I couldn't say that I blamed him.

Guys like Beck getting a scholarship was like a slap in the face to those of us who couldn't afford it.

"You play?"

"Yeah." He nodded and his signature grin was back on his face. "I'm not half bad."

"What's up, Hollis?"

I tensed as I heard his voice far too close to me. Will looked up with a smile on his face, and I continued to stare straight ahead as they slapped hands. I couldn't see him, I didn't dare turn in his direction, but I could smell a hint of his cologne. It somehow was so much darker than Will's. Where Will was the sun, Beck was smothering.

His mere presence all-consuming.

"Hey, man. You slumming it on the beach today?" Will chuckled, but I had no doubt that Beck rarely spent his spare time hanging out on the beach with the Clermont High students.

"Something like that." I could feel him staring at my back, but I didn't care. I took another long drink from my cup, and I could barely taste it. I was too aware of him. Too anxious with him standing behind me. "I see you met Vos's sister."

I winced as he said my last name. I looked up at Will, and I could tell hearing my last name made things different for him. I didn't know what it was. My dad's money or that he knew my stepbrother, but there was an instant difference to him. Just like there had been with Beck.

But Will didn't hate me.

"I didn't realize you were Lucas's sister."

"Step," I clarified quickly, but Beck scoffed.

I finally looked up at him, and I instantly wanted to slap that small smirk off his face. He looked so at ease, so at peace with his hate for me, and I had no fucking clue what his problem was.

"It's nice to see you again, Vos." He looked me over, not hiding one moment of him perusing my body, not from me and definitely not from Will.

"Don't call me that." I shifted on my feet and his eyes stayed glued to my thighs at the movement.

Under all that hate, there was the edge of lust in his gaze. Just that small look made me feel crazy. It made the memories of the other night come crashing back into me.

It didn't matter how much I had tried to bury them.

"Will?" Beck ignored me and looked up at Will. "Do you mind giving me and Vos a moment alone?"

Will looked between the two of us as if he was missing something, as if I had lied about not really knowing him. "Sure." He smiled at me again, and I wanted to tell him not to leave. Instead, I wanted to tell Beck to go to hell, but I didn't do either.

I watched Will walk away, back toward the bonfire, then I stared daggers at Beck.

Those flutters in my stomach became a hurricane, and it shook through every part of me.

"What's your problem?" My tone was sharp.

There was a spark in his eyes, something that told me I shouldn't fuck with him, or maybe that no one ever had, but I didn't care. He didn't even know me.

"My problem?" he asked with a false calmness to his voice, but there was nothing calm about his eyes. The hazel looked as golden as the fire that danced next to him. He looked every bit the king that these people thought he was. He looked every bit the devil. "What's your problem?"

The rational part of me was long gone. I didn't know what it was about him, but he infuriated me.

"You're my problem." I stepped closer to him, and his eyes flicked to my mouth. "I don't know what your problem with Lucas is, but I'm not him. You don't even know me."

He looked back up at my eyes, and he looked hungry.

It was like whatever I had just said only seemed to fuel him.

"I know you, princess." He reached his hand out, and I held my breath as he moved a piece of hair out of my face. My heart was hammering in my chest. I should have slapped his hand away. I should have shoved him or screamed or told him not to touch me, but I didn't do any of those things.

I just watched his eyes as his skin grazed against my own,

and my blood boiled at the way my body reacted. My body remembered every filthy word he had sent me the other night.

It remembered every illicit touch he had provoked.

"You're a Vos."

"And you're a Clermont," I snapped with as much venom as he had.

He cocked his head to the side and watched me. I squirmed under his scrutiny. I hated the way his eyes were studying me. I hated the way a simple look could make me feel so much.

"If you know so much about us Clermonts, then you know we don't fuck around. I told you to quit the country club."

"And I told you to fire me."

I didn't know why I was pushing so hard against him. I could have just backed down and laid low, but I refused to take shit from anyone.

If he expected a doormat, he came for the wrong girl.

He stepped closer to me, and I willed myself not to move backward even though the urge was overwhelming. As harmless as Beck seemed to everyone else, I could see the fury he hid behind his eyes. It was dark and unending, and I knew it would be relentless if he unleashed it on me.

I only had a taste.

But I didn't care.

Fear would only go where I allowed it, and I had no room for it here. Not when he would use it against me.

His chest brushed against mine and the hurricane in my stomach felt like it was falling lower and lower. I had no interest in whatever game he was playing, but I refused to back down. I stared up at him, a good foot over me when he was standing this close, and I prayed he could see my own fury staring back at him.

I hoped he could see that I wasn't one of these people who was going to roll over just because he deemed it so.

But he wasn't looking at my eyes.

He was staring at my mouth, and he suddenly looked like a different guy standing in front of me. The fury was still there, but it was clouded by something else. Something that reminded me of an animal that could eat me alive.

This was neither the guy on the beach nor the guy who wanted to destroy me.

"You smell good." He pushed another piece of hair out of my face, but this time his thumb trailed down my neck and I knew he could feel my racing pulse.

I felt like I had whiplash from his change of pace, but I refused to let my guard down around him. That was exactly what he wanted.

"You don't." It was a lie. The intoxicating smell of him was deceptive. It put me at ease, like a clear night sky when all you could see was the stars. It was just another thing about him that was meant to trap you. To make you forget about the danger that hid just beyond your view.

But even knowing that, I couldn't stop myself from breathing him in. He was so close, and even though I knew he was dangerous, I just wanted a glimpse.

Beck Clermont was nothing but cruel, but he was thrilling.

"You wound me." He placed his hand over his heart, and I saw a sliver of his tattoo peek out from the edge of his t-shirt. The urge to find out what it was, was overwhelming. "Most girls tell me how much they love the way I smell."

He was so cocky, so sure of himself, and I was sure that most girls did. But I wasn't most girls.

"I'm sure they tell you lots of things you want to hear." I straightened my spine and looked around. Almost everyone was near the fire, leaving Beck and me alone, and I hated that an ounce of fear ran through me. Beck was powerful when it came to Clermont Bay, and I didn't want to know how far that power went. I didn't want to know what he was capable of.

The malice he had already shown me was enough.

"But not you." His chest rose and fell against mine, and I was sure that anyone who was watching us would think we were the opposite of what we were.

"Not me."

I held my breath as he lifted his hand toward my face, and I could feel my knees shake as he ran his thumb over my bottom lip with a roughness that I felt all the way to my core.

Every time I had seen him, even through his cruelty, he had always been so obsessed with my lips. He was constantly looking at them and touching them when he had the chance.

I should have been repulsed.

What I shouldn't have been doing was having the sudden urge for him to kiss me. It was crazy. I wasn't an idiot. I knew exactly what kind of guy Beck was, but I still wanted him to kiss me.

My body pushed farther into his, and I swear I didn't know how it happened. One moment I wanted nothing to do with him, and the next I felt like I would die if he didn't do something. I squeezed my thighs together, begging them to stop the ache that pulsed between them, and I stared up at the guy who hated me.

And I could have sworn he wanted to kiss me too. Even with my lack of experience, I knew a guy didn't look at a girl like he was looking at me if the only thing he wanted from her was for her to leave.

His hand touched my waist, half on my shirt, half on bare skin, and I didn't dare look down. His fingers dug into me as if he was trying to hold me away from him while simultaneously wanting to pull me closer.

The arrogance in his gaze was gone, slipped away without his approval, and what was left behind was someone I felt desperate for. For a guy so confident in who he was, he looked lost, and it fueled me to think that I could have been the one thing to do that to him. That I could make him lose himself in a world that was built to satiate his every need.

I ran my tongue over my suddenly dry lips, and he watched the movement as his hand tightened against my waist. There was an edge of pain in his touch, and I knew I should have wanted it to end. But I didn't.

"You're fucking trouble." He spoke as if he wasn't even talking to me, as if he was simply thinking out loud, and I wanted him to say more.

"I'm nothing." I shook my head. I was nothing to him, and I didn't know if I was trying to convince myself or him. Whatever this was, it was nothing.

"You are." His hand held me even tighter. The pain of Beck's fingers like a brand on my skin. "You're the same trash as your brother."

He let me go, his hand acting like my center of gravity at my waist, and when his skin left mine, I felt like I was going to fall.

He stepped back from me, the lost boy from moments before buried beneath the guy he was now, the guy he always was.

He stared down at me with clear disgust on his face, and I didn't know if he was revolted by himself or by me. But I knew with certainty that the moment where he looked like he could possibly want more from me was gone.

He didn't say another word as he turned from me and made his way back to where his friends still stood. They were watching us, they probably had been the whole time, and I suddenly wondered if they hated me too.

Allie had told me that the three of them were more like brothers than friends, and I could tell by the way they still had their eyes on me as they laughed at something someone said that they didn't trust me.

But I didn't trust them either.

I didn't trust anyone who could allow their friend to be so cruel while they simply sat back and watched.

I lifted the shitty beer to my mouth, and I swallowed every drop as I stared back at them. I didn't care that Clermont Bay was their kingdom. I refused to play by the rules of a few privileged boys who thought they ran everything.

They were madness, and I refused to be a pawn in their game. Whatever it was that they wanted from me, they would have to get it from somewhere else.

I could already feel the one beer buzzing through me, or maybe it was still the effect of having Beck so close, but I knew that it was a feeling I didn't want to let go of. Not yet. I poured another beer from the keg, and I downed half of it before I managed to move my feet back to where Allie stood.

She was still talking cheerfully with some of her classmates, and she grinned as soon as I made my way to her side.

"What was that about?" She bumped my shoulder, and I knew she meant Beck. She was as shocked as I was by his behavior at the country club, but for some reason, I didn't want to tell her the truth. At least not all of it.

Not the part where I stood there like a fool while I half-expected him to kiss me.

"I don't know." I shook my head and took another sip of the beer. "I think he might be insane."

She laughed and crashed her cup into mine. A bit of beer spilled over the side, and I tried to relax. I could avoid Beck and his friends for the rest of the night. I was here to enjoy my night with Allie, and I was determined to do so.

Even if I could still feel him looking at me from across the bonfire.

"Here." Allie handed me a small flask. "This will help you forget all about him."

It was like she was reading my mind. I took a small sip from the flask, and I coughed as the rich liquor burned my throat.

It tasted worse than the beer. Allie grinned and patted my back.

I could feel the alcohol buzzing through me as the night went on, but I didn't stop. Beck tracked my every movement, but I didn't care. I laughed with Allie and made lots of new friends, even though I couldn't remember their names, and I was pretty sure I barely even looked over at him or the girls who were vying for his attention.

I barely noticed the smirk on his face when he saw me watching him or the way that damn smirk made my stomach feel so tight that I couldn't clear him from my thoughts.

I had no idea what time it was by the time Allie grabbed my arm in hers and giggled. It was beyond clear that the two of us would be Ubering home.

"Beck is looking at you again." She rested her arms on my shoulders and looked behind me to where I knew he still stood.

"He can keep looking." I actually sounded like I meant it.

"He looks like he wants to eat you alive." She swayed slightly, and I barely managed to hold us both up as my thighs tightened. "It's kind of hot."

"It's not hot." I lied to both of us. "It's neurotic."

"Uh-huh." She sounded like she didn't believe me at all, and I didn't blame her. I didn't even sound believable to my own ears.

"Do you just want to stay the night at my place?" I didn't want to go home alone tonight. I wasn't sure if Lucas was even there, and I didn't want to sit in my room and dissect every single moment I had with Beck.

"Sure. Your parents won't care?"

My heart cracked open at her words. My mom would have cared. She would have given me a speech about responsibility while simultaneously trying to get any juicy details out of me about my night.

"No." I shook my head and finished my beer. "My dad probably won't even be there."

"We need to call an Uber." She poked the tip of my nose, and even though I wasn't used to having such a close relationship with another girl, I felt so comfortable with Allie so quickly.

"I'll give you all a ride." I turned my head to the left, where Will stood now covered in a t-shirt. He had barely spoken to me since Beck interrupted us earlier, and he hadn't looked at me the same.

I hated Beck even more for that.

"Thank you." I had barely managed to speak the words before I felt him at my back.

"Allie, me and the boys will give you all a ride home."

Allie smiled up at Beck as he spoke, and I tried to catch her eye. *Tell him no.*

But Allie wasn't looking at me. She was staring up at him like he had just offered her the moon.

"Thanks, Beck. That would be amazing."

I dared to glance over my shoulder, and he was still smiling at Allie. He glanced from her to me, and I knew from the spark in his eyes that I shouldn't go anywhere with him. Whether I was drunk or not, I didn't trust Beck Clermont.

"Will actually already offered to take us." I turned so I was facing Beck more, and Allie snickered in my ear.

"Will's been drinking." Beck tucked his hands in his pockets, and he looked so damn smug.

"Only a couple." Will shrugged, and I knew I wouldn't be riding home with him tonight. Even if I absolutely despised the idea of Beck being my ride home, I wasn't stupid enough to get in the car with some guy I had just met who had been drinking.

I wasn't that reckless.

"I haven't had any." Beck shrugged his shoulders with a

cocky smile, and I wanted to knock that damn smug look right off his face.

"I think we'll take our chances with the Uber." I tightened my grip on Allie, and I couldn't stop smiling as she laughed.

"Or I could call your dad." Beck pulled his phone out of his pocket. "I think he'd much prefer it be me to get you home safely than some college student trying to make an extra buck."

I narrowed my eyes at him, but I didn't doubt he'd do it. "You wouldn't dare."

"Try me, Vos." He tapped his thumb against his phone.

"There's no need for that." Allie linked her fingers in mine and squeezed them before she spoke. "We'll ride with you, Beck."

He didn't look at her though. He stared down at me, and I swear he wanted me to challenge him. There was a dare in his eyes. "You good with that?"

I wanted to say no. It was on the tip of my tongue, but Allie squeezed my hand tightly in hers and I took a deep breath as I stared at him. "Perfect."

CHAPTER EIGHT

BECK

J osie looked pissed as hell as she climbed into the back seat with Allie.

I couldn't stop smiling as I shut the door behind her.

"What the hell are we doing?" Olly was standing near the hood of my SUV, and I knew he thought I was crazy.

I didn't give a shit though.

There was something about her that made me crave being near her. I wanted to crush her, but I wanted to do it where I could see. I wanted to do it where I had a front-row view.

"Taking two drunk girls home safely." I tossed my keys in the air and caught them back into my hand.

"You know that's not what I mean." He looked between me and Carson, but Carson knew as much as he did.

They were my best friends, more like brothers, really, and while I knew they hated Lucas Vos as much as I did, it wasn't the same.

They were close to Frankie, but she wasn't their baby sister. They didn't have to watch her helplessly as she cried like I hadn't seen since she was a little girl. They could see how she's changed since that day, but I could feel it.

I felt every second of it, and it burned in my blood.

"Just get in the fucking car, Olly."

I opened my driver's side door and climbed in. Josie sat directly behind me, and I couldn't help checking my rearview mirror as soon as she was in view.

And she was staring daggers at me.

She was pissed, that much was obvious, but there was no way I was going to let Will Hollis take them home. I had been watching him drink all damn night, and more than that, I had been watching him watch her.

I shouldn't have fucking cared.

But for some stupid reason, I couldn't let her leave with him.

The thought of her smiling at him like I had seen her do

when I arrived at this stupid fucking party made me want to smash Will's face in.

That anger was irrational and dumb, but Josie was mine. My want for her felt carnal and predatory.

Allie's head was resting on her shoulder, and she was clearly already passed out. Allie was fun. I had always liked her since she had started working at the country club several years ago, but she also had a bit of a wild streak.

That fact always seemed to bug the shit out of Carson, but he never acted on it. If he was really into her, he never made a move.

Right now, he sat beside her and stared down at her like she had pissed him off beyond measure tonight, but the two of them barely even spoke.

That guy could have any girl he wanted, and he did, a lot. But he was always staring down Allie like she had robbed him of all the pleasure in life.

I wanted to say that was part of the reason I offered to take them home, but it would be a lie. I only fucking cared about Josie.

I would use Allie in whatever capacity I needed to get under Josie's skin. Carson would just have to be pissed about it.

He could hate me if he needed to.

I drove to Josie's house which wasn't far from my own, and no one said a word. I could tell she wanted to, but she held her tongue. I wondered if she would have, had we been alone. Or would she have lashed out at me like I was the last person she wanted to be around?

I put the car in park and started to climb out.

"I got it from here." Josie nudged Allie in the side as she unbuckled herself.

I leaned my head back into the car and stared at her. "You going to carry Allie in?"

She wasn't listening to me though. She shook Allie's shoulder, trying to wake her, and I waited. Allie looked like she was completely dead weight, and I had half a mind to watch her struggle to carry her inside.

Josie and Allie were roughly the same size, with the exception of Josie's soft curves, and I knew there was no way in hell Josie would get her in the house.

"Carson, carry Allie." I shut my front door to end any argument she may have had, and I took a deep breath before pulling her door open.

Carson already had Allie in his arms, but I wasn't looking at them. I was staring down at Josie as she glared up at me.

"Do you need me to carry you too?" I cocked my head to the side, and I knew the moment the question passed my lips that it would piss her off.

Good.

I wanted to piss her off.

I wanted her to fight me.

"If you fucking touch me, I'll kick you in the balls."

I grinned as she scooted out of her seat, but I didn't give her any space. I stayed exactly where I stood, my back against the door, and I waited for her to climb past me.

She was stubborn, but I would be unmovable.

"Excuse me." Her knees pressed against my thighs as she remained perched on the edge of the seat to get out.

I didn't budge. I stared down at her, and I waited for her next move.

She huffed and her cheeks reddened when she realized I had no intentions of just letting her pass me by, and she slid from her seat. Her body touched mine, and I knew she hated it. I didn't. All of my blood went straight to my cock at the small feel of her. She tried to slide by me, but I reached out my hand and stopped her. I knew that asshole was in the house.

In her house.

And knowing he was so close, made me want to break something. It made me want to break her.

"Let me go, Beck."

"And if I don't?" I cocked an eyebrow and moved closer into her space. She smelled so good, but it wasn't some expensive-ass perfume like most of these girls wore. It was something else. Something innocent and addicting. Even her scent begged me to ruin her.

"I'll scream."

As she said the words, her body moved the slightest bit closer to mine. Regardless of what she thought she wanted, her body felt differently.

Her breathing was faster than only moments before, and I couldn't stop the urge to touch her. It was overwhelming.

The compulsion was all-consuming.

Lucas Vos could look out his window and see me touching her. He could watch exactly what I would do to her body.

I gripped her chin in my hand and forced her face to look up at me. I knew my grip was too tight, but I couldn't stop it. I couldn't be gentle with her.

I refused.

I pulled her face closer to mine, and I could see the edge of fear in her eyes. They were clouded with lust, but her anxiety was still clear. "Did you scream the other night when you did what I told you to do?"

Our lips were so close to each other, and all I had to do was lean forward a fraction of an inch and I would have her. There wasn't an ounce of resistance in her body. She wanted me as much as I wanted her. She wanted me as much as I wanted to destroy.

I wanted to taste her to see if the memory of her was accurate.

But I wouldn't give her that.

She would have to beg me, and even then, I didn't know that I would give in to her. Regardless of how badly I wanted to.

"I didn't," she said it like she meant it, but she was lying. There was a spark in her eyes and a flush on her chest that told me so. We both knew it too. I could smell the alcohol on her breath. I had watched her drink all night. She wasn't as drunk as Allie, but she wasn't completely thinking clearly either.

"You sure about that?" I trailed my hand down her throat, and I thrived on the sharp inhale of her breath. She didn't move except for the rapid push and pull of her chest, and I felt mesmerized by the movement. "Did you imagine it was my hand on your pussy? Did you fight against it or were you so willing to let me have you?"

My thumb traced her collarbone as she shuddered, and I wished it was my tongue. I bet she tasted as sweet as she smelled. I bet she would squirm under my tongue and beg me for more.

And I would make her beg.

My fingers ran over the swell of her breast, a barely-there touch, but it was enough to unnerve her.

"What do you think you're doing?" Her voice was shaky as a tremor ran through her chest.

"Whatever the fuck I want." Her eyes snapped to mine, and her anger returned full force.

She pushed past me, and I grinned. My cock was so hard against the zipper of my jeans. I pressed my hand against it to adjust myself before I closed the door behind me and followed her step for step. She almost tripped on the sidewalk, but I caught her around her waist.

"Don't touch me." She barely looked over her shoulder at me.

I lifted her in my arms and her body stiffened slightly. She was still dead weight in my arms, the alcohol too much for her to overcome. "What are you doing?"

"Carrying you inside before you trip and kill yourself."

She rolled her eyes, but she didn't fight me. She laid her head back and looked up at the stars like she couldn't care less if she was in my arms.

"You're an asshole." She blurted out to the sky, but I knew she was talking to me.

"I've been told that a time or two," I muttered, but she wasn't listening to me. She was lost in her own little world.

"But you're a beautiful asshole." She looked from the sky to me, and I knew it was the alcohol talking now. She would never admit such a thing without liquid courage.

"You think I'm beautiful?" I teased, but she just rolled her eyes again.

"You know you're beautiful." She lifted her hand and slapped my cheek playfully. "It's your fatal flaw."

"My beauty?" I chuckled.

"Your arrogance." She blinked up at me. "My stepbrother has it too."

I hated that she compared me to him. I fucking despised it. I was nothing like that piece of shit.

"Your stepbrother has more than one fatal flaw then." If she thought his arrogance was the worst thing he possessed, then he had her fooled. But I knew she couldn't be that far in the dark. I knew she had to be aware of the demons that hid in her house.

"He's not as bad as you think he is." She let her head fall back again.

She was wrong.

She was so fucking wrong, and my heart pounded in my chest as she defended him.

We reached the door, and I pushed inside. Joseph Vos was nowhere to be seen, but I wasn't surprised. I rarely saw the man here when I was still friends with Lucas. If I did, he was always on the go.

Her father wasn't the kind of man that could stay in the same place for long.

I shifted her in my arms as I climbed the steps.

"You hate me because of him. Don't you?"

I looked down at her, and she was staring straight back up at me. There was a look in her eyes that I couldn't quite place, something that dared me to be honest with her, but I refused to let my guard down because some pretty girl was in my arms and looking at me like she needed me.

Especially some pretty girl who was nothing but a pawn to me.

"It doesn't matter." She shook her head, and it took everything in me not to kiss her. Her bottom lip had the perfect little arch, creating a shadow beneath, and I wanted to run my tongue across it. I wanted to run my tongue across every damn inch of her.

I made it to the top of the stairs, and I stopped in my tracks as I stared at Lucas's open door. He stood there in nothing but a pair of sweatpants, and I was certain that he had been asleep before we arrived.

He ran his hand through his blond hair, then his sleep-filled eyes opened in shock as they met mine. I stepped forward with his sister in my arms, and I couldn't stop the way my hands tightened around her.

My fingers could have been bruising her, and I wouldn't have cared.

Whatever chance she had of escaping me was long gone the moment he looked down at her in my arms and I saw fury take over his features.

I ate it up, the feeling of power it gave me. I had barely even touched his sister, but he didn't know that. All he knew is that she laid in my arms like she fucking belonged there, and she was staring up at me like she never wanted to leave.

She was staring up at me like she felt more at home in my arms than she ever would in these fucking tainted walls.

But he knew better.

He knew that I would use her in any way I needed to fuck with him. To pay him back for what he did to me. For what he did to *her*.

"What are you doing here?" His words were threatening as he stepped toward me, and I prayed he came closer. I prayed the motherfucker gave me the slightest reason to wreck his face again.

"Just taking care of your sister." I cocked my head to the side as he stared at her in my arms.

He took a step closer to me and held out his arms as if I would ever just hand her over to him.

"I've got her." He nodded his head, but he was out of his damn mind.

I would have never given her to him, especially not with the way she clung to me. Not with the way she was begging me with her eyes not to let her go. The tips of her fingers were turning white with the force of her hand clinging to my chest.

"That's not going to happen." I stepped to move past him, and he blocked my path. If she wasn't in my arms, I would have knocked that damn look off his face, and no one would have been able to stop me. Not like last time. They would never have been able to pull me off of him again. "Get out of my fucking way, Lucas."

"What are you doing with her, Beck?" His nostrils flared, and his chest puffed as if he was going to do something about it.

He had the nerve to act like he fucking cared.

Lucas didn't care about anyone but himself. We both knew that.

He had proven it to us both.

"That's none of your business." I tightened my hold on her. "What I do with her is between me and her."

Her fingers spasmed against me as her body squirmed.

My cock strained against my jeans, and I wanted to do everything to her. Everything.

Especially when I looked at the fury on Lucas's face.

"Let him go and go to your room." He spoke to her as if he was her real brother or even her father. He spoke to her as if he knew her intimately.

And it only made me want to destroy him even more.

"Get out of my way, Vos. I won't tell you again." I meant it too. We both knew it. We both knew that I would seize any opportunity to take a shot at him.

He backed out of my way, but he stood by her door watching me. I didn't give a shit. He could watch whatever the fuck he wanted. He could watch while I destroyed his sister the way he had mine. While I destroyed him.

Carson had already laid Allie in Josie's bed, and even though he would never admit it, I knew that he had been so gentle with her and tucked her in like she was the most precious thing on Earth. Even if he was currently staring down at her like he hated her.

I sat Josie on the edge of her bed, and I looked around as she balanced her hands on my shoulders. Her room looked nothing like her. It was frilly and posh, and she was, well, she was the exact opposite.

I barely knew anything about the girl, and even I knew that.

I pulled her shoes from her feet and dusted sand from her legs as she stared down at me.

"Should I pull these off too?" I tugged on the edge of her shorts, my fingers grazing her thighs, and she stiffened.

"Don't even think about it." Her words were firm, but her body squirmed gently beneath my hand.

"One day." I laughed and noticed Lucas still standing at the door staring me down. I leaned closer to her as she scoffed, and I held his gaze.

"I told you that was never going to happen." She looked up at me, and I hadn't really noticed until that moment how the brown of her eyes was encased in swirls of green. They were enchanting and vulnerable and absolutely nothing like Lucas's. But that didn't matter. It couldn't matter.

Josie Vos was the key to everything. I couldn't touch Lucas without her.

And even though she was looking at me like she trusted me more than she ever should, I couldn't let it fuck with my head.

I couldn't let some pretty girl fuck with my plan.

"I guarantee it, princess." I nipped at her earlobe, and she released a sharp inhale that was equal parts shock and lust.

I had planned to make her life a living hell from the moment I spotted her at the country club, and I would. But she was going to make it much easier than I thought.

She wanted me, regardless of what she was telling herself, and I would use that knowledge to my advantage.

I would use her, and I would make every moment of it worth it.

CHAPTER NINE

JOS!E

There was a pounding in my head that I couldn't ignore. It seemed to block out everything else. My alarm was going off somewhere in the background, but I didn't care. I just wanted it to stop. The blaring, the pounding, the sudden wave of nausea.

Shit. What the hell was I thinking last night?

The pounding fell away as memories of the night before bombarded me. Memories of me drinking, of Beck, of him carrying me all the way to my damn bed.

Nausea hit me again. This time harder.

I had let him carry me through this house and to my bed. I clung to him. I had wanted him.

Oh, God.

I blinked my eyes open, and Allie was still dead to the world next to me. Her blonde hair was stuck to her face, and she let out the tiniest little snore. I would have left her there, let her not have to worry about how she felt for a little bit longer if the two of us didn't have to be at work.

With customers and food and Beck. I hoped to God he wouldn't be there. I didn't want to see him. Not today, not ever again if I was being honest.

If we could just avoid each other altogether, that would be for the best. Because Beck Clermont confused me.

He hated me.

He said so. He looked at me like he did.

But there was some part of me that thought it was more than that. There was a part of me that thought maybe his hate was just a mask for something else, and that part was dangerous.

Whatever reason he had to hate me was completely lost to me. But if there was one thing I was sure of is that he did.

Even if there was more. Even if I was insane and thought that he could possibly want me.

He hated me more.

And I was going to be attending school with him in a couple of weeks. A school that I knew he ruled. A school where he could make my life a living hell.

There was only one solution when it came to him.

I needed to put my head down and avoid him like the plague. I needed to avoid him at all costs.

Or I would have to deal with the consequences, and I wasn't prepared for that.

I had a plan.

And that plan did not include some privileged boy who hated me for no reason.

Regardless of how incredibly handsome he was. And he was. He was the most beautiful guy I had ever laid eyes on. But it was all part of who he was.

It was part of this damn persona that he portrayed.

I needed to keep my head down, study my ass off, and save as much money as I could for when I left here. I wanted to go to college. I wanted to become something more than a sum of my past and my father's last name.

I shook Allie, trying to wake her up, and she groaned. I knew she was probably feeling doubly as bad as I did. Allie had far more to drink than me. She wasn't even awake when we arrived back at my house.

I was so glad my dad wasn't here. Not that he could say anything.

But Lucas had plenty to say.

I could have drunk the entire keg, and I would have still remembered his face when he saw me in Beck's arms.

He looked like he was going to be sick before his anger took over.

It should have made me push Beck away and never look back, but it didn't. I just clung to him harder. I clung to him as if he was some sort of savior.

And Beck Clermont was the farthest thing from that.

Deep down, I knew that.

"We have to get ready for work." I nudged Allie's arm, and she groaned again.

"What the hell happened last night?" She rolled over onto her side to look at me, and I couldn't stop smiling at the way she barely had one eye open as if that was all she could manage.

"We drank too much." I chuckled, and she put her hand on her forehead.

"Yes. Yes, we did." She pushed up on her elbows and looked around my room. "How did we even get back here?"

She was clearly much drunker than I had been. Maybe it would have been better if I didn't remember. If I didn't remember the way he looked at me or the way he touched me. Holy shit. He touched me. He grabbed my jaw and bit my ear, and I had done nothing but look up at him like I wanted more.

Oh, God.

"Beck and his boys brought us here." I groaned. "After you accepted his offer to drive us."

She dropped onto her back again and threw her arm over her eyes. "Sorry."

"It's okay." I laughed and pushed to my feet. We were going to be late if we didn't start getting ready.

"Did I make a fool of myself?" She looked genuinely worried, like she cared what the three of them thought about her.

"No." I shimmied out of my shorts and threw them in the corner of the room. "You were asleep for most of the ride, and Carson carried you up here."

She shot up then, as if I had told her that she ran around the party naked. "He did not." She looked horrified.

"He did." I nodded my head. "I was too tipsy to even try to get you up here."

"Oh my God." She buried her face into the bed and growled out a scream.

"Should I have not let that happen?"

"It's fine." She stood up and pushed her hair out of her face. "I've just known Carson a really long time, and I'm sure he loved watching me be a mess."

"When you say you've known Carson, you mean?" I cocked my head and studied her. She seems far too affected for it to just be that.

"I mean that Carson isn't really my biggest fan. We'll leave it at that."

I was dying to know that story, but I wouldn't pester her about it. If she didn't want to tell me, she didn't have to. There was plenty I kept from her.

I hadn't even told her about my mom. I hadn't told her anything, really.

But it had been so long since I had really talked to anyone about anything. Not anything that actually mattered, and I wasn't ready to do so here. I wasn't sure if I ever would be.

The two of us scurried around the room getting ready, and I lied to myself as I put more makeup on than normal. I told myself that I needed it due to the night before, but I knew I was anxious about the possibility of seeing Beck today. Surely, he wouldn't be there.

Didn't rich boys get to spend their summers sleeping in and not worrying about clearing their hangovers off as quickly as possible for work? I knew Lucas did.

He didn't have any obligations or responsibilities outside of the baseball workouts that he attended through the week.

By the time we made it to work, my headache was just a low roar, and Allie looked like she had a perfectly peaceful night of sleep. I wasn't sure how she did it, but she somehow looked incredible.

I hated her for it.

Our shift was busy, the two of us had sections right next to each other, and as each hour passed, I started to calm my nerves. Beck wasn't going to be spending his weekend at his dad's company.

He had far better things to do. He was probably off with his friends or off with some girl.

That thought shouldn't make me feel anything, but it did.

It made me feel insanely jealous over a boy who I shouldn't be feeling anything for.

By the time our shift was ending, I was exhausted. I wanted nothing more than to climb into bed.

"Josie, do you mind running this food to Mr. Clermont's office?" I looked up at one of the cooks, then looked around me. The other servers were still tending to tables, but this was the absolute last thing I wanted to do.

"I don't know where it is."

He looked annoyed, but I didn't care. I had no interest in spending any time with any of the Clermonts if I could help it.

"Straight down the hall and to the right. It has his name on it. You can't miss it." I grabbed the bag of food from his hands and pushed out of the kitchen with a huff.

It was already ten o'clock, and I couldn't believe that Mr. Clermont was still here. I wondered if he was a workaholic like my father. I guess, to have an empire like his, he had to be. The men of Clermont Bay were basically all the same.

Money and power were more important to them than anything else.

I didn't have to know much else about Mr. Clermont to know that.

I reached his office, and I stopped short when I heard voices inside. The door was cracked, and I didn't know if I should knock or just set the food outside the door. I raised my fist to knock, then I heard it, Beck's voice, and I took a sharp breath.

I had no interest in seeing him.

Especially not in his father's office. Not after a day like today. Not after last night.

"I'm not firing the girl because you have some imaginary problem with her." His father's voice rang through the office, and I leaned closer to the door to listen.

I knew it was wrong, but I didn't care.

"You know why I have a problem with her." I could hear the anger in Beck's voice. "The only people who are imagining things are you and her damn father."

Were they talking about me? They had to be.

"Don't lump me together with that man." Mr. Clermont left no room for argument, but Beck didn't care.

His voice was sharp as he snapped at his father. "Then don't act like him."

"Son." His dad hesitated, his voice eerily calm, and I wished I could see his face. "It's time for you to start acting like a man."

I covered my mouth with my hand, and I hated that I was still standing there listening. I should have given them their privacy. I knew that, but I wanted to know more.

If this was the only way that was going to happen, then so be it.

My heart raced as I eavesdropped on their conversation, and I looked up and down the hall. There was no one there to catch me for what I was doing.

No one would know.

"You're going to be taking over this business soon, and I can't leave it in your hands if you're going to be more concerned with holding a grudge than you are with running this place."

Beck was going to be running this business? I figured that would happen eventually, but I thought he'd be going to some Ivy League college, where he drank far too much beer and hooked up with more girls than I could imagine.

Rich boys didn't go straight to work out of high school.

There was silence in the room, and I had no idea what was

happening. I couldn't see a damn thing through the crack, and I really didn't want to get caught. I raised my hand to knock just as Beck's words rang through the room.

"I will destroy them."

"And her?"

"Josie Vos is the perfect fucking pawn."

I stepped back from the door and took a sharp breath as my heart skipped over itself. I didn't know why I was so shocked by his words. He had been cruel to me since the moment I met him, but last night... Last night nothing changed, and I was a freaking idiot.

I rapped my knuckles on the door, not waiting for either of them to answer. I didn't care if Mr. Clermont owned this place or this town. I refused to sit out there and listen to another moment of their conversation.

Both of their gazes swung my way. Mr. Clermont was sitting behind his desk, and Beck stood across from him with his hands buried in the back of the leather chair. His dad painted a gentle smile on his face, but Beck wasn't nearly as practiced. Or he simply didn't care.

His anger was pure and unadulterated, and I could feel it as if it was a living, breathing thing.

"I brought your dinner." I stopped at Mr. Clermont's desk and set it in front of him. I didn't meet his eyes. Mr. Clermont was a mystery to me.

He seemed so different from the other men in Clermont Bay, but my father seemed different to others as well. But I knew the truth. These men had a lot of experience when it came to their facade.

They were nothing more than snakes hiding in plain sight. At least with Beck, I knew where he stood. At least with him, I knew the danger that laid at my feet.

I knew that he would strike at any moment.

"Thank you, Josie." His father smiled before his gaze

jumped to his son, then back to me. "I hope you're having a good evening."

"Yes, sir." I stepped back, and I avoided looking anywhere near Beck even though I could feel him staring at me.

"How are you liking it here so far?"

I knew he was just making small talk, but I couldn't stop myself. Beck had just been talking so openly about how much he hated me. He hadn't cared at all.

"It's been fine." I smiled at him. "Some are more welcoming than others."

Beck scoffed under his breath, but I still didn't look at him. That was exactly what he wanted.

And I refused to give him anything that he wanted anymore.

If he wanted me as his enemy, that was fine. I could play that part perfectly.

If that's who he wanted to make me, that was exactly who I would become.

"Has my son here been one of those unwelcoming people?" He chuckled, but I could see the tension around his dark eyes. Eyes that matched his son's.

I should have said yes. I should have told him that his son was a complete and total asshole, but I didn't. That was what Beck expected me to do, and I was tired of being what people expected.

"No." I shook my head. "Your son has been so nice." I still didn't look at him, but I knew he was looking at me. He always seemed to be looking at me.

"My son?" He chuckled again, and this time it sounded genuine. He didn't expect my response either.

"Yes, sir." I smiled. "Tonight is mine and Allie's trash night, and he offered to help."

Beck made a sound that made it clear that there was no way

in hell as his father looked back and forth between the two of us.

"I know what you're thinking." I pushed my hands into my apron pockets to stop myself from fidgeting, and I finally stared at Beck. He looked so handsome, even just standing here in his father's office wearing a plain white t-shirt and a pair of dark jeans. "I was a bit shocked, too, when his highness offered to help, but apparently he's willing to get his hands dirty."

So was I.

I didn't say it out loud, but I hoped he saw it in my eyes. He was staring me down, still angry, but I didn't care. I could handle his anger.

His dad laughed, a full-on belly laugh, and I pulled my attention from Beck long enough to look at him. He was probably about to fire me for insulting his son, but I suddenly didn't care.

"His highness." He laughed again, and I tensed. Did I really just say that out loud? "Well, please don't let me get in your way." He motioned toward the door. "Beck, it seems like you have some trash duty to attend to."

"It would be my pleasure." Beck pushed away from the chair, and I swallowed hard as he walked past me. He looked more pissed off than I had ever seen him. He looked like he was ready to strike at any moment.

I smiled at Mr. Clermont before turning and following Beck out the door. I didn't know what I had expected after I said that, but it wasn't for him to actually do it.

I had expected him to push back. I had expected and wanted him to fight me. I was craving a fight.

I closed the door behind me and stared at Beck who leaned against the wall across from me. He looked like he wanted to say something. I was dying for him to say something, but he just glared.

He was angry, but he also looked like he was hungry. He looked like he could devour me in a moment's time.

And even though I had no experience when it came to the matter, I still wanted to know what it would feel like.

The thought of being devoured by someone like Beck made me lose my breath.

"What game are you playing?" He cocked his head to the side, and a rush of fear ran through me.

"I'm not playing a game." I pushed my hair out of my face and walked away from him. He may have had time for this sort of thing, but I didn't. I actually did have a job to do.

I felt him behind me a moment before his body hit mine. I was too shocked to say a word. Too shocked to do anything as his body pressed into my back.

His left hand gripped my upper arm as if he thought I would run away, but I was stuck to the spot. With his harsh breath on my neck, his hard body behind me, I could barely think, let alone move.

"What the fuck do you think you're doing, Josie?" His mouth was near my ear, and the memory of him biting the sensitive flesh came back full force. I squirmed, attempting to put some space between us, but he held me tightly against him.

And I felt every inch of him against me as if there was nothing separating us.

I took a sharp breath as I felt his hard erection at my lower back, and I could practically feel his smile against my neck.

"I need to get back to work." I barely recognized my voice.

"Hmm." His lips vibrated against my skin, and I tried to catch my breath. My chest was vibrating with something: fear, anxiety, anticipation. I didn't know which, but I knew that I couldn't get a deep enough breath to think straight. "You think you'll get fired if they know where you are."

His hand tightened on my arm and his other hand snaked around the front of my neck. His fingers pressed into my tender skin, and I knew he could probably feel my erratic heartbeat hammering against his fingers.

Regardless of how I tried to act, he could feel every bit of how nervous he made me.

"If they knew that I was touching you in the halls where anyone can see."

I hadn't even thought about that. I try to move out of his hold, but he dug his fingers tighter against me. He had no intentions of letting me go.

Not that easily.

"Let me go, Beck."

He gripped my chin in his fingers, and I winced at the force of his hold. "Say it like you really mean it, and I will." His body somehow seemed to get impossibly closer. I couldn't stop myself as I reached behind me and gripped his thigh to hold myself steady. If he noticed, he didn't let it show. "Say it like you don't want me to take you into the next room and fuck you hard against the wall."

The sound of my breathing was the only thing I could hear.

I had never been touched like this, never spoke to in such a way that I couldn't even concentrate.

"Let me go."

I knew the moment the words passed my lips they were no more convincing. I wasn't even convincing myself. Not with the way his middle finger drew small circles against the rapid pulsing in my neck. I could practically feel that exact movement between my thighs.

"Say please." His left hand gently moved down my arm at a lazy pace, and I looked down and watched as it barely missed the side of my breast. He was teasing me. Logically, I knew that, but I didn't want him to stop.

I was an idiot, but his hands felt too good and the throbbing between my legs seemed to be the only thing I could think about.

It didn't matter that his dad, my boss, could catch us at any second. It didn't matter that anyone could. I just wanted him to touch me. To give me more.

His hand skimmed from my arm to my stomach, and it trembled beneath him. He was barely even touching me, his hand on my stomach a stark contrast to the hand still holding my face, but I could feel every small inch of movement as if it was being burned into me.

He toyed with the buttons of my shirt, the movement of his fingers captivating every part of me before he'd stop, and I couldn't stop the way my body arched into his touch, silently begging him for more.

He gave me what I wanted, the slightest amount more than the moment before, then he would take it away. A push and pull. A chase and torment.

His fingers pushed harder, the tips touching the top of my pants, and I couldn't stop the soft whimper that left my lips.

What the hell was happening with me?

I knew I shouldn't want him with absolute and complete certainty, but I did.

I wanted him more in that moment than I had ever wanted anything else.

"Please," I said it so quietly, but I knew he heard me.

His breath was harsh against my neck, and it did nothing to help the way my heart hammered against my chest. I tightened my hand on his thigh, and I barely knew what I was asking him.

I wanted more. I needed more, but I didn't have a clue what more entailed. More had repercussions. Repercussions that I would have to face.

"Say it again." He breathed the words against my neck before his tongue touched the skin just below my ear.

"Please, Beck." I was firmer this time. I was sure. I didn't know anything about the guy who stood behind me other than his social standing and his hatred for me, but I still wanted him.

He moved his hand then, beneath my apron, the heel of his palm pressing against my sex, and I was wrong when I imagined my hand was his. He had barely touched me, and already my hand hadn't compared.

He cupped me over my pants, but it felt like there wasn't a thing between us.

He moved his hand in small circles just as his tongue flicked against my pulse point, and I bit down on my lip as I whimpered.

He followed suit and bit down on my neck.

"Oh, God."

His hand sped up, and my legs felt like they were going to give out beneath me.

"You want this?" His breath was harsh against my neck as he ran his nose along the slope.

I nodded my head and chased the feel of his hand with my hips.

"I need your words, princess. Tell me you want it."

"I want it." My response rapidly fell from my lips. "I want you."

He was gone in an instant. The feel of his body behind mine, nothing but a memory, and I almost fell backward in his absence. I had been so lost in him that I had forgotten the force that kept me rooted. I had forgotten everything that didn't begin and end with his hands.

He moved across the hall, putting distance between us, and if it wasn't for the storm brewing in his eyes, I would have thought him completely unaffected. His mask perfectly in place.

"You should get back to work." He jerked his head toward the direction of the restaurant, and I took a step back at the sharp edge to his voice.

I wanted to say something, I needed to, but I couldn't find my voice. I couldn't find my voice or my thoughts or the sense I needed to tell him to go to hell. All I could do was stare at the asshole who I had just practically begged to touch me.

He looked calm as hell, like his hands hadn't just been toying with every damn part of me, and I suddenly hated him more than I ever had before.

Whatever Beck's problem with me was inconsequential. I didn't need any of his stupid reasons or unresolved entitlement. I wanted nothing more to do with him.

I steadied my breath, and I took a step away from him with determination not to look back. He had me exactly where he wanted me. He was in my head, and guys like Beck knew exactly what they were doing.

He knew exactly how to play any game he wanted to.

But I refused to play.

I was only here for one school year. A school year where I would put my head down, get my high school diploma, and get as far away from this place as I could.

Get away from these men who thought their money somehow made them untouchable. Get away from it all.

"Josie." I stopped as soon as my name fell from his lips. Every bit of resolve I just felt disappearing at the sound of his voice. I didn't dare look back at him because I wasn't sure what I would do. I wasn't sure if I could handle looking in those fucking eyes for another second without forgetting who I was.

His footsteps echoed through the empty hall, and I knew he was making his way back to me. I should have left. My feet should have moved, and I should have left him standing there wanting more.

But I couldn't.

Walking away from Beck Clermont was impossible. He was the bad guy, I knew that, but no part of me seemed to care.

Because I stood there in anticipation of what he would do next, of what he might say.

He pushed some hair from my shoulder, exposing my neck fully to him. "I love that you were willing to beg me."

Shame shot through every part of me at his words, but he didn't care. Beck would never care, and I had been an idiot to want any part of him.

He moved past me, not sparing another glance my way, and he disappeared as if he was nothing more than my imagination.

But I wouldn't give him that advantage again. I would never see Beck for anything other than exactly what he was. He was the villain, ruthless, cruel, and I was nothing more than a game to entertain himself with.

I refused to be taken captive in his game again.

CHAPTER
TEN

BECK

"Who pissed you off tonight?"

I stared up at Olly and took another drag from the joint. I almost never smoked, but I needed it tonight. I needed something to take the edge off before I went fucking crazy.

Before I went back to the country club and fucked the shit out of Josie Vos.

I had thought of nothing else since I walked out that door.

I had been there to do the exact opposite. I didn't have the power to fire her, not yet at least, but I couldn't imagine how my father could just waltz around there with a Vos shoved right under his nose.

I understood that he was a businessman, but this didn't feel like business. It felt like he was laying down and letting Joseph Vos fuck him in any way he wanted.

I wasn't my father. I refused to let Joseph Vos or his fucking son get away with anything else, and I wanted to take out every bit of my anger on her pretty unmarred skin.

She had been so pliable in my hands tonight. I knew she had wanted me as badly as I wanted her.

Her body admitted it as easily as her mouth had.

Every stroke of my fingers had her body begging for more. I felt powerful with her under my touch. It fueled me and fucked with my head.

The need to use her barely outweighed my need to taste her.

But it had to. I couldn't lose sight of who she was. No matter how enticing she was, she was a Vos, and nothing else mattered.

"Beck." I looked at Olly and tried to remember what he had asked me. Had he asked me something?

"Yeah?"

He pulled the joint from my hand and took a long drag before releasing the smoke. "This must be some good shit, huh?"

I nodded and chuckled. I was barely even feeling the weed. I was still too fucked up on her.

"The girls are here." He nodded to the door, and I watched as Cami and her posse of rich, entitled girls pushed through the party like they owned the damn place.

She looked the same as she always had, and if it had been only a few days earlier, I would have even said she looked beautiful. But that word tasted wrong when it came to her.

Cami wasn't beautiful.

In looks, God, yes. She was smoking hot, and she knew it. But that was half the problem, Cami's ego was the only thing that could compete with her insecurities, and she used both to keep her rank in our world. She used both to put people in their place.

And to make sure they stayed there.

But very few of them actually knew her. Not really. Not like I did.

But she did let me see her. Every part of her.

I was one of the only ones who knew about her fucked-up affair and how she let Mr. Weston use her whenever he wanted.

It had all become a part of this fucked-up game she seemed to be playing. She let him use her while she used everyone else.

But she hadn't used Frankie.

Cami stepped in front of me, her smile wide and her eyes a little wild. I was sure that she had been drinking or smoking. She rarely went a day without it, and I wasn't one to judge her for it.

If there was anyone who demanded excellence for Cami more than she did for herself, it was her parents, and that demand took its toll on her.

So did the fact that the man she loved went back home to his wife every night.

You couldn't tell unless you knew where to look. Unless you watched as the spark in her eyes slowly faded.

"Beckham." She leaned down, putting a hand on each of my knees. I should have been affected by her touch; I used to be. But somehow, I couldn't bring myself to feel anything for it now.

Not after Josie.

"I feel like I haven't seen you in forever." She moved her finger back and forth over my knee, but I didn't move an inch. I just stared into her eyes and waited for her next move. Cami always had her next move planned out in her head.

"I just saw you the other day." I motioned to Olly, and he passed the joint back as he spoke to one of Cami's girls. I drew the joint to my lips, and Cami tracked the movement. She licked her lips and my dick jerked. Regardless of where my head was, he hadn't forgotten her or that mouth of hers.

It knew me better than most of the people at this fucking party.

And it always came back to me when she needed me. She came back whenever he pushed her away.

"It feels like a lifetime ago." She leaned forward and her lips pressed against mine with no preamble. She didn't wait for permission or even a flicker of want from me, she didn't need it.

She had never needed it before.

I opened my mouth, letting the smoke gently flow from me, and she breathed it in like she was dying for it.

That was the thing about Cami. She was always dying for something.

Power, admiration, drugs, love. They all amounted to about the same to her.

"I'm really not in the mood, Cami." I pushed her away from me, and there was a slight moment where I saw the doubt in her eyes, the edge of panic.

I almost never pushed her away. No one did. If Cami wanted it, she got it.

It was as simple as that.

But I wasn't in the mood for her tonight. I wasn't in the mood for any of these people.

"You know our senior year is about to start." She said it so quietly and sweetly that I knew others probably thought she was whispering something dirty in my ear.

All Cami ever whispered was dirt. Dirt on her enemies and her friends, and dirt that helped her keep her secrets safe.

I looked up at her, and I wondered if I looked as bored as I felt. "I'm aware, Cami."

She smiled at someone who walked past us, but I didn't glance their way. I cared even less about them than I did her.

"Then don't forget our arrangement."

She stared into my eyes, and I wondered what she was going to do when she left this party. I wondered if she would fuck him as soon as no one was wondering where she was. "I haven't forgotten."

"Then look like you're fucking happy to see me." She leaned forward again, and she pressed her mouth back against mine.

All I could think about was Josie. How soft she was and how sweet she smelled. She was the exact opposite of Cami. Anyone who saw them could tell that within a moment's notice, but I also knew that Josie wasn't nearly as sweet as she led everyone to believe.

I stood up, forcing Cami to step back, and I pushed past her without another word. I wasn't here tonight to make these people look at us. I didn't give two shits what they thought. I made that very clear last year.

When they all thought it was wise to fucking talk about my sister.

When they thought they fucking had the backbone to whisper her name. I shut that shit down before it could even echo off the walls.

She was the only one I cared about out of all these people.

Her and Olly and Carson. They were my family. All of these other people were just noise.

If Cami hadn't been so good to Frankie, if Frankie didn't care for her so much, I would have cut her off just like the rest of them.

My phone rang in my pocket, and I glanced down at Frankie's picture before I quickly answered.

"Hello."

"Hey, Beck. What are you doing?"

I ran my hand through my hair. I didn't really want to tell her I was at a party, but I wouldn't lie to her. "I'm at Josh's house."

She knew exactly what that meant. Josh was a party boy, and no one would even be here if it wasn't for the epic parties he threw constantly.

"Oh. Okay." She hesitated, and I hated that she did. I hated that any part of her had been diminished. "I'll let you go."

"No." I said it so quickly I had no doubt I shocked her. "What are you doing?"

"I'm just hanging at the house. Me and Mom were watching a movie, but she's already passed out."

I laughed because that's how our mom always was. I don't think the woman had ever finished a movie if it was after nine o'clock. I had watched my father carry her to their room more nights than I could count. Back when he could still do so.

"You want to do something?" I pulled my keys out of my pocket, and I was already on my way out the door. I would drop anything for her.

I would do anything.

"No. You enjoy the party."

"I'm already heading to the car. Let's go for a swim." It was one of her favorite things in the world to do. It always had been.

"It's already eleven." She rustled around, and I wondered if she was already in bed.

"So? Get ready and grab my shorts. I'll be there in fifteen."

"Are you sure?" There was a spark in her voice that told me she was excited, and even though once upon a time, I was a shitty brother who would have taken that sound for granted, I didn't anymore.

"Yes, Frank. I'd much rather hang with you than these assholes."

"Okay." She laughed. "But stop calling me Frank."

She didn't mean it. I had been calling her that since we were little, and I was the only one she allowed to do so.

We hung up the phone, and I started climbing into my SUV just as Olly came jogging from the house.

"You leaving?"

"Yeah. I'm going to go hang with Frankie."

I didn't know what it was about him and her, but he took last year almost as hard as I did.

"I'll go with you." He climbed into the passenger seat before I could tell him differently.

"Where's Carson?" I started the car and pulled off. Carson rarely left a party unless it was with a girl.

"He was making out with two different girls when I left."

He wouldn't be missing us then.

Olly and I barely spoke on the way to my house. He seemed stuck in his own head, and I knew that I was stuck in mine.

Frankie stood outside as we pulled up, and there was a bit of shock in her eyes as she watched Olly climb out.

"Was the party that bad?" She laughed, but she knew as well as I did that Olly didn't give two shits about that party. He wouldn't have even been there if it weren't for me and Carson.

"A complete bore." He chuckled and tucked his hands in his pockets as he stared at her.

It was weird.

The way the both of them were looking at each other was fucking weird.

"Let's go." I linked my arm in hers and led her through the back gate. We passed by our perfectly clean pool, the lights shining brightly beneath the water, and I unlocked the gate at our property's edge.

The smell of saltwater was so clear and pure, and Frankie and I both took a deep breath as our feet hit the sand. The ocean was black with a sliver of moonlight dancing across the surface.

The water was harsh and deep, and God only knew what hid beneath the surface, but this beach and this water had been an escape for Frankie and me ever since we were old enough to go to the beach alone.

It was our place.

It didn't matter who else was with us. It belonged to the two of us.

Frankie squished her bare toes in the sand, and I kicked off my tennis shoes and threw them to the side. Olly was standing beside her doing the same, and he was still watching her. I didn't know what he expected her to do, but he didn't seem to be able to look away.

I threw on the shorts she brought me before grabbing her hand and walking into the water with her. A year ago, she would have run headfirst into the water without a worry in the world, but that time was gone.

That wasn't who she was anymore.

She hadn't been that girl since Lucas fucking Vos.

My hand tightened on hers, and I tried to calm my temper as she looked up at me. I couldn't think about that asshole without an all-consuming rage.

He had been my friend. I had fucking trusted him.

I trusted him.

And I regretted every moment of it.

If I didn't know that it would hurt Frankie, I would kill the motherfucker. I had thought about it more times than I could count, but it would hurt her.

I had hurt her already when I had let my rage take control, and nothing mattered to me except not letting her get hurt again.

Not by anyone, but especially not from him. I refused to even allow him to look her way. It killed me that he was going to be in the same school as us this year. He should have been kicked the hell out. His ass shouldn't be breathing the same air as her. She should have never had to look at him again, let alone go through the school year like everything was okay. Like nothing ever happened.

She let go of my fingers as the cool water lapped at our knees, and the urge to reach out and put her hand back safely in mine was overwhelming. But she looked so happy out here in the water. Her smile was genuine for the first time in a long time, and she dove into the water as if there was nothing to fear.

Olly jumped too, staying right by her side, and I pushed out into the water until it hit my chest. I stared out over the dark water and tried to think about what the hell I was doing.

My senior year was about to begin, and I should be thinking about college. I had been offered a handful of scholarships on baseball alone, but I didn't need any of that. My parents would pay for whatever school I wanted, but I only had one choice. The local university was my only option with the way my father's health was deteriorating. It didn't matter that he said differently.

It was clear just looking at him.

He would need my help much earlier than any of us thought, and it didn't matter if this wasn't what I wanted. It was what I was destined for. Clermont Bay was laid before my feet, and I would be a fool if I didn't realize the privilege my parents afforded me.

It didn't mean that I still couldn't hate it.

It didn't mean that I couldn't be thankful and dreadful at the exact same time.

Because I was.

I didn't know how my dad did what he did every day. He was much stronger than I would ever be, than I could ever amount to.

I could see someone walking down the beach, and I tensed. There was rarely anyone on this beach as they all had private entrances from the homes that took up residence here. Old money. That's what rested on this long boulevard. If you didn't have it, you weren't welcome.

Those weren't my rules. It was just the way things worked. They had been that way forever.

I watched the figure get closer and closer, and my heart hammered in my chest. The Vos's home was only a few houses away from ours, even though it felt like there were miles between us.

If I brought Frankie out here and that bastard was to walk by, I wouldn't be able to control myself.

"Who is that?" I turned back to Frankie, and she was mostly blocked by Olly's body. But I could still see a small jolt of terror that tore through her.

"I don't know." I pushed myself back toward the beach. "I'll check it out." I looked at Olly, silently telling him to watch out for her, and he gave me a look back that I knew meant he was offended that I felt the need to say anything.

He would protect her as wholly as I would. He wouldn't let a thing happen to her.

I stepped out of the water and moved down the beach as I clenched and unclenched my hand. Water was dripping down me since I didn't dare stop for a towel, but I didn't care. The breeze was cold, but I welcomed it.

I stopped in my tracks as soon as I could see the figure enough to know it wasn't a guy. Instead, there was a girl moseying down the beach with a book in her hand and her eyes on the water. She didn't once look around her, not an ounce of self-preservation visible.

I watched Josie's dark hair blow in the breeze, and she bent down to pick up something out of the sand. She hadn't even spotted me coming closer to her, and somehow that fact pissed me off more than the thought of her brother.

This girl lived with two fucking devils and she still walked through the dark as if there was nothing to fear. It was the same way she looked at me. She looked at me like she didn't care that I was the villain in her story, and I would take advantage of that fact. I would take advantage of every error she made.

I was only a few feet away from her when she finally looked my way. She jolted back as if I shocked her, and the fear that flushed her face in the moonlight gave me far more pleasure than it should have.

"What are you doing?" She stood, her fingers covered in sand, a dull seashell in her hand.

"What are you doing, Josie?" I pushed my hair out of my face and water trickled down my hand. She stared at me as if she was watching every fraction of movement it made. There was no shame in her gaze. She openly gaped at me as her eyes slid down my body.

She didn't look like a girl who hated me.

Not at all.

She looked like a girl who was staring at something she couldn't have.

Because no matter how gorgeous she was, she couldn't have me. No matter what I led her to believe.

No matter how badly I wanted her.

She pulled her gaze away from me and looked down at the book in her hand. "I was just going for a walk."

"In the middle of the night?"

Her fingers tightened around the paperback. "You're out here in the middle of the night."

"Not by myself."

She looked behind me as if she hadn't realized anyone else was out here, and I hated that her lack of self-preservation bothered me so much. She stepped back, looking back to where her house stood, and I should have let her go. I should have let her walk away and head back into her nest of vipers.

But there wasn't a single part of me that wanted to let that happen.

I had her within my grasp. In the middle of the night, my prey was staring up at me like she wanted me to strike. It was as if she was begging me to make my next move.

I gripped the edge of her book and pulled it from her hand. She gasped and tried to snag it before I could get too far, but she didn't stand a chance. She jumped at me, trying her hardest to get the book back, but I held it higher, completely out of her reach.

"Stop, Beck." Her chest pressed into mine as she tried to fight against me.

"The Duke that Saved Me." I read the title of the book and couldn't stop laughing as I looked at the cover. "Josephine, you little scandalous thing."

The cover was tattered, and it was clear that the book had been read time and time again.

"I swear to God, Beck. Give it to me right now."

I didn't listen to her. I flipped open the book and read a line aloud. "Her hands trembled as she fumbled with his buttons. Not only was he her first, but he was also her only."

Her elbow smashed into my ribs, and I groaned as I leaned forward, knocking myself farther into her. Her cheeks were stained red as she snatched the book out of my hand.

"I didn't realize you were such a dirty girl."

She huffed and tried to push away from me, but I pulled her

closer. I may have been her enemy, but that didn't mean I didn't like the feel of her against me. I could afford a few moments of her skin against mine.

She was so warm and soft, and even though she pretended like being next to me was the absolute last place she wanted to be, she was pliable under my hands.

"This was my mother's book." She said it like it was somehow supposed to make a difference to me.

"Your mom is a dirty girl too?" I licked my lips, but she froze. Everything that was soft about her moments before had now gone hard.

"Don't talk about my mom." She pushed against my chest, and I let her. Even though it was the last thing I wanted. I stumbled back a couple inches from the force of her hands.

"She was with your dad, right? She can't be all that innocent." Because anyone who was a Vos was evil to me.

"Well, she's dead." Her voice shook, as did her hands.

I stepped back and tried to think of what to say. I didn't know. I had not a single clue. If I had, I would have never said what I had just said. I may have been cruel, but I wasn't that cruel. I wasn't so fucked up that I would tease her about her dead mother.

"I'm sorry. I didn't know." When everyone had been talking about Joseph Vos's daughter that had arrived in town, they said they thought she had been sent to her father because of her behavior. She was his black sheep.

His fucking blemish on his otherwise perfect life.

I didn't know the truth.

"Why would you know that?" She took two steps back, and her face had morphed from sadness into anger. "It's none of your business."

She had a point, but people in Clermont Bay made a life out of knowing everyone else's business. Normally, I would have known everything about her by now, but it seems Joseph Vos was keeping more than one secret.

"It's not, but I'm still sorry. I wouldn't have said that."

"Wouldn't you?" She cocked her head to the side and held the romance novel to her chest as if it was the most precious thing in the world to her. "Let's not try to fool each other here, Clermont. You're as cruel as the rest of them."

She was right. I was. I would use her to get my revenge on her family, and I wouldn't feel bad about it. I had decided the day I first met her that I would refuse to feel anything other than hate.

I had already let that slip with the way I wanted her physically. I refused to let it go to anything beyond that.

I refused to let her convince me to not use her. I would. I just hadn't figured out how yet. I had thought that being cruel to her like Lucas had been to my sister would have set him off, but he had barely reacted.

Unless she hadn't said anything to him.

But I didn't suspect that to be true. This town had secrets, but everyone still whispered. Nothing truly stayed secret for long. Everyone had their own version of how things went down. Even if it wasn't the truth.

The truth rarely mattered. Not when there were plenty of lies to cater to what they wanted. To what they cared to believe.

"I am." I watched her mouth as she pulled her bottom lip into her mouth. "But I wouldn't have been cruel about that."

"Hi." I jolted forward as my sister's voice sounded from behind me. I had almost forgotten that they were still back there. "I'm Frankie."

She smiled at Josie, but Josie was still looking at me like I had ruined her entire night. She looked at me like I had wanted her to only moments ago. Like I was the villain.

"Hi." Her voice was shakier than before. "Josie."

"I remember you." My sister's voice was calm and kind, and

I didn't know how she could stand here and talk to the sister of the guy who had ruined her life like that.

I didn't know how she wasn't screaming like I had heard her do night after night.

"I met you at the club," Frankie reminded her. "It has to suck being around this one all the time."

Josie laughed as Frankie nodded her head toward me.

"He is a bit much." She didn't even glance in my direction as she spoke about me.

"That's putting it mildly." Frankie bumped into my side gently. "I'd say he's an asshole a good fifty percent of the time."

"That too." Josie smiled and tucked her hair behind her ear before she looked behind her. "I should really be getting back home."

I could tell she felt uncomfortable with the two of us. Olly was still wading in the water behind us.

"Do you want one of us to walk you?" Frankie asked, but I already knew the answer.

"No." Josie finally looked at me, and the hostility instantly came back in her eyes. If she didn't hate me before tonight, before everything I had done, she did now. "I'll be fine. It's not far."

"I'd rather walk you." I took a step toward her, and she took a step back.

"And I'd rather you not." The false calmness she held in her voice since Frankie arrived was now gone. She didn't care who heard her or the way she felt about me.

"Why don't you at least let Beckham walk you to the back of your property? It will make me feel better."

Josie looked like she wanted to tell her to go to hell, but she didn't. She nodded her head once, then took a few more steps away from me. "It was nice to officially meet you, Frankie."

"You too."

She didn't wait for me. She took off in the direction of her house, and I followed behind her step for step.

"I really am sorry."

She huffed and started walking a bit faster.

"I don't need your fake-ass apologies."

I sped up, trying to look at her, but she looked out toward the ocean. "I wouldn't have said it if I didn't mean it."

Her head jerked in my direction. "And what about earlier? Do you want to say you're sorry for that?"

I knew exactly what she was referring to. She wanted an apology for the way I touched her earlier. She wanted me to say sorry that I turned her on and made her ask me for it.

I wouldn't though.

I wasn't sorry for a second of it, and I wasn't lying when I said that I wouldn't say it if I didn't mean it.

"I'm not sorry for that." I shook my head and watched her anger rise. "I'm just sorry we didn't get to continue."

She stepped toward me suddenly and a wave of her sweet scent washed over me. "That will never happen again."

"It will." I pushed a piece of brown hair off her shoulder, and her chest rose and fell like the ocean behind her. She could lie all she wanted about what happened earlier, but we both knew she wanted me.

Even if I hadn't noticed her chest, it was impossible to ignore the way her eyes clouded over when I stood this close to her or the way her lips opened just slightly.

It was enough to make me want her just as badly. It made me want to prove to her how easily it could happen again.

"You think that you can have anything you want." She had so much volition as she spoke. She meant what she said. Every single word of it. She truly believed that she could stop anything from ever happening between us. "But you are not a fucking god, Beckham."

I hated that my sister had used my full name in front of her. No one used my full name outside of my family.

"You'd be shocked to learn what I am, princess."

"Don't call me that." She didn't look like she wanted me to stop calling her that. She looked like it made her want me more.

"Or what?" I couldn't stop testing her. The thought of her pushing back, of her fighting me, it turned me on far more than anything else. Even more than the way her fingers dug into the book or the way her bare feet pushed into the sand as if she was trying to get herself closer to me without taking a step. "What the fuck will you do about it?"

I touched her collarbone with the edge of my fingertip, my touch barely a whisper, but it felt like I was screaming at her. I was begging her to make me stop or make me go further.

If she made me stop, if she pushed me, I would only push harder.

"What do you want from me?" She was staring up at me, and I knew that she would let me take this further. If I wanted to, I could easily lean forward and take her mouth. I could take anything I wanted.

"I haven't quite figured that out yet." I was lying straight through my teeth. I wanted to taste every single bit of her, then I wanted to ruin her. I would. Regardless of the way she was looking up at me or the lecture I knew Frankie was bound to give me once I got home.

I moved my finger from her collarbone to her neck, and I loved the way I could see her pulse hammering against her tan skin. I made her nervous.

"Well, I'm not here for you to toy around with while you figure it out." She lifted her hand and slapped my fingers away from her skin. "You can go fuck yourself."

I wanted to reach out and stop her. She was here for whatever I wanted her to be. We both knew it.

But I let her go instead.

She looked back at me as she pushed through the gate at the back of her property, her mansion of a house towering over us.

I knew that Lucas and her dad were probably both in there, and they probably didn't even have a clue that she was gone.

I wondered if she was as disposable as everyone else in their life.

She shared Joseph Vos's last name and his blood, but I wasn't sure that any other part of him ran through her. She seemed so different from the rest of her family, but I wouldn't let that stop me.

I was already too far gone, and nothing could stop me at this point.

CHAPTER
ELEVEN

JOSIE

I could hear yelling the moment I woke up. I pushed the hair out of my face and sat up.

My father's voice was practically vibrating off the walls. He was angry. That much was perfectly clear.

I pushed out of bed and looked at the time. It was seven o'clock in the morning, and I had only been asleep for about five hours. I couldn't sleep after I got back to the house last night.

A run-in with Beck on the beach was the last thing I expected, and it kept replaying over and over in my head every time I tried to sleep. His annoyingly handsome face kept appearing no matter how much I told myself that I needed to hate him.

The yelling was getting louder, and I opened my door to see what the hell was going on. I saw no one in the hall, so I took hesitant steps toward the staircase.

"I don't give a shit what you think, Lucas. It's not your place to think anything."

Lucas's mom, Amelia, said something back to my father, but it was too quiet for me to hear. I leaned over the stairwell and there they all stood in the foyer. Lucas looked like he had just got home, and I was almost certain he was drunk.

"So what, you got your daughter home and now you don't give a shit about me anymore?" His voice was sharp and full of venom, and my heart skipped when he mentioned me.

"My daughter isn't your concern." My father stepped toward him, and if I was Lucas, I would have cowered away. I may have hated my father, but even I wasn't stupid enough to not see how intimidating he was.

"But she is." Lucas stumbled slightly on his feet. "She's been hanging out with Beck Clermont. Did you know that?"

My breath caught in my throat. *What the hell?*

I hadn't really talked to Lucas since the night we ran into

him in the hallway, but I had thought we were closer than him talking about me to my father behind my back.

"He brought her home the night before last."

"You knew she would be around him. She's working there." My father's voice was even lower than before. I had no idea what their problem was with Beck, but it was clear that there was one.

"Since when does the boss's son carry girls home drunk from work?"

That fucking traitor.

"What's the issue with Beck Clermont?" All three of their eyes snapped up to me as my heart raced. I knew what my issue was, but I wanted to know theirs. I needed to know.

"Oh, Josephine, you're awake," Amelia said as calm and nice as could be, but I didn't care what she had to say.

"There is clearly an issue."

My father straightened himself, becoming the perfect image of put together, and attempted a small smile. "There is no issue."

"I'm not an idiot." I waved toward his drunk son. "Lucas hates Beck, and Beck clearly hates Lucas."

"What the hell did he say now?" Lucas bit out, he had never spoken to me that way before.

"He didn't say anything." I crossed my arms over my chest and made my way down the stairs. It was a lie, but it wasn't. He had admitted how much he hated Lucas, but none of them had told me anything. "He didn't have to."

"He's trash," Lucas spit. "That entire family is trash."

"You're drunk," I said out loud what everyone else was thinking. "I think you may need to sober up."

"Fuck you."

My heart ached as I looked into his blue eyes that were so full of venom and anguish.

"Hey." My father jerked him by the arm and forced him to face him. "Don't talk to her like that."

I hated that he was defending me. He had never defended me before, and I didn't need his help now. "It's fine. He doesn't mean it."

I hoped he didn't mean it.

My father stared at me, his eyes were the perfect twins to mine. I could see the storm brewing beneath the surface, and I knew he was probably looking at the same thing in mine.

"Why don't we eat breakfast?" Amelia was still trying to calm the situation, and I felt sorry for her. Here she was with her asshole husband and drunk son who was acting like an even bigger asshole, and I wondered if this is what her life had been like.

She was beautiful, but there was an edge of sorrow in her eyes.

"I'm not hungry." Lucas pushed past me, his shoulder brushing against mine, and I could smell the liquor on him. Whatever Lucas did last night, he went hard.

"Get your shit together, Lucas." My father's booming voice stopped him in his tracks. "Senior year starts in just a few short days, and I expect you to act like a Vos."

I knew he was talking to him, but I felt like he was directing that at both of us. Like he expected me to act like that name was supposed to mean something to me.

Lucas didn't reply. He forced himself up the stairs, his anger still radiating off him, and I actually felt bad for him even if he was being a jerk.

Joseph was my father, but I hadn't had to deal with him like Lucas had. I hadn't had to live up to any of his expectations because he didn't have any for me.

When Lucas was out of view, my father's attention turned to me. "I gave you my permission for you to work at that country club, but I don't want you to hang out with Beck Clermont."

I could have told him that I wasn't. That Beck hated me as much as they hated him, but I refused to.

He may have been my father, but he wasn't my parent. He didn't get to slip into my life and suddenly tell me what to do.

"I'll hang out with whoever I choose."

"No. You won't." He grabbed his suit jacket off the table and slipped his arms inside. "This year is important for you. You live under my roof now, and you'll follow my rules."

What he meant to say was that this year was under his control. He hadn't given a shit practically my entire life, but now he thought he could dictate what I did or didn't do.

"What's wrong with Beck Clermont? Tell me, and I won't hang out with him again."

Amelia wrung her hands together and looked back and forth between me and my father. Whatever reason they had to hate Beck, it wasn't something that was going to go away any time soon.

"I thought you were friends with Mr. Clermont."

"We're business associates," my father corrected, his tone brokered no room for argument. "And I bet that Mr. Clermont would agree that the two of you have no business being around each other."

He grabbed his keys and his wallet, and I knew he wasn't going to discuss this any further. My father thought that his word was gold and expected everyone to obey him.

He expected wrong.

I didn't plan on having anything to do with Beck, but it wasn't because my father had ordered it so.

That only made me want to get to know him more. It made me die of curiosity to know why the hell they hated each other so much.

"I've got some meetings this morning." He tucked his phone in his pocket. "I'll see you all at dinner."

He wouldn't be seeing me. If I wasn't at work, I would eat

my dinner in my room. I refused to sit around a table with them and pretend like we were some happy little family.

I didn't respond to him, but Amelia kissed him and wished him a good day. I couldn't stop myself from rolling my eyes.

I walked away before he could say another word. The kitchen counter was covered in food, and I smiled at the cook my dad had here several days a week. It still made me feel awkward, and I hated that there was someone here to serve me.

I knew these people were all used to it, but I was not. Nothing about this felt normal to me.

"I can make you something if this isn't to your liking." Her smile was warm and reached her eyes that were touched by age.

"This is more than enough." I grabbed a couple of waffles before loading them down with fresh fruit and syrup. I started to walk back to my room, but at the last minute thought better of it. I pulled out one of the chairs at the island and sat down across from where she stood.

"I'll give you your space."

"No. Please, stay." I cut into my waffles. "Have you eaten?" I motioned toward the food, and she looked at me like I was crazy.

"I'm fine. Thank you, Josephine."

"Josie," I corrected her. "What's your name?"

"Liz."

"It's nice to officially meet you, Liz." I stuffed a bite of the delicious breakfast in my mouth. I may not have liked being waited on, but I couldn't deny the woman could cook.

"You too." She folded a dish towel and straightened it out on the counter. "Are you ready for the school year to begin?"

I don't know what it was about her, but there was something that reminded me of my mother. There was something about her that made me feel more at home than anyone that lived in this house.

"Not really." I laughed. "I'm not used to going to a school like that. Plus, I know no one."

"At least you'll have Lucas."

I made a face at her, because there was no way in hell that she didn't overhear that conversation, and she laughed quietly.

"I'll pick up your uniforms in the next couple days."

Ugh. I totally forgot that they all wore pretentious uniforms. "Yay."

She leaned onto the counter, her fist resting under her chin. "Clermont Bay Prep is a good school. A lot of people would kill to get in there."

I was such a spoiled little brat. "I know that. I don't mean to sound ungrateful." I pushed some hair out of my face. "I just never thought this is where I'd end up."

She looked at me with so much sympathy on her face that I knew she knew about my mother. There was no way that she didn't. "I'm sorry about your mother."

Her words stabbed through my chest. No one had said those words since I had been here. Technically, Beck had said them last night, but that was out of guilt.

She was the first one who had genuinely been sorry for my loss.

I hadn't even felt like my father cared.

"Thank you." I stared down at a strawberry and pushed my fork into it slowly.

"I know how hard it is to lose your mother." Her voice sounded distant, but I couldn't stop myself from looking up at her. "I didn't lose mine as young as you, but the loss of your mother is something you will never get over. But it will get easier."

My chest felt like it was going to cave in on itself, and even though I appreciated what she was saying, I also desperately wanted her to stop talking. The only way I didn't feel over-whelmed by my mother being gone was to not think about her at all. But it never seemed to work. Something always reminded me of her.

"Thank you." It was the only thing I could think to say. "I miss her."

"I know you do." She moved around the kitchen a bit. "But you owe it to her to live a wondrous life."

My gaze snapped up to hers.

"I obviously didn't know her, but that's what I want for my children. I want their lives to be wonderful and filled with love."

The thought of Beck popped into my head, and I forced it back. I didn't like Beck Clermont. He was a carbon copy of the men I had sworn I wouldn't allow to control my life, and he was just as cruel as they were.

"What do you know about the Clermonts?" I blurted out my question before I could think better of it, and she looked a little shocked. I couldn't blame her.

"They're a nice family." She searched my eyes. "Why do you ask?"

I looked over my shoulder, but there was no one there. Amelia always seemed to disappear the moment my father was gone.

"I'm sure you heard all that this morning." I motioned to the foyer where my father had been yelling. "I just don't understand what their aversion to the Clermonts is."

"Are you curious about all of the Clermonts or just one?" She raised an eyebrow, and I knew my face flushed red with embarrassment.

"Well." I pushed my food around on my plate. "I would like to know why they specifically hate Beck so much."

Liz sighed and leaned back against the sink. "Beckham used to spend a lot of time here."

My breath caught. *He spent time here?* I was shocked by that information.

"He and Lucas and those other two yahoos he runs around with were close friends."

"What happened?" I pushed to the edge of my seat. I would have never guessed that any of them had been friends. Not with the way they hated each other now.

"I don't know." She shook her head. "They were all over here one day, then the next, poof. No more. Lucas hasn't been the same since then though." She tapped her fingers against her thigh. "I really shouldn't be telling you any of this."

I knew she probably feared my father just like everyone else, but I needed more information. I needed to know what happened.

"They just stopped being friends?"

"I'm sure something had happened." She shrugged. "But whatever it was, I didn't hear about it. I only hear things your father is okay with me hearing."

I knew exactly what she was saying. These walls held secrets. Secrets that weren't just held from her but from me too. Secrets that kept my father thriving.

"Beckham is a good boy though. He has always been kind and respectful."

I felt like she knew another boy entirely. I would never describe Beck as either of those things.

"But I would stay away from him if that's what your father wishes. He must have his reasons."

Yes, he must, but I wasn't important enough to know what they were. Whatever Beck had done, my father didn't want me anywhere near him.

Whatever had happened, it had turned a group of friends into enemies. If Liz was right, whatever had happened between them had to be bad.

Friendships didn't end over simple misunderstandings.

Either Lucas or Beck had done something. Maybe they both had.

The boys of Clermont Bay weren't to be trusted. Not a single one of them. If I was smart, I would hide away from all of them. I would spend my year with my head down and my mind clear. But Beck had no intentions of letting that happen.

I wasn't disillusioned enough to think that Beck was doing anything more than using me as a part of whatever the hell game he was playing. But even having that knowledge, I was a fool. Because there was a part of me that wanted to surrender to him.

My heart hammered in my chest violently, and I knew that I had no choice.

Beck Clermont would use me however the hell he wanted.

CHAPTER
TWELVE

JOS!E

School started tomorrow, and I should have been preparing.

I knew that, but I didn't want to think about it.

Going to that school meant I wouldn't be able to avoid Beck.

I would be in his element, in his kingdom, and there wouldn't be a single place to hide.

But I couldn't think about that today.

When Sam, the manager of the golf course, had begged for someone to pick up a last-minute shift on the course after someone called in, I quickly volunteered.

I needed the money, and I needed the distraction.

"I'm going to have you working at the desk this morning." He ran his gaze over me. Sam was attractive. He was older than me, sure, maybe by half a dozen years or so, but he still had a boyish charm about him that I doubted he would ever lose.

I followed him through the club, having never really been to this side before, and I absently thought about Beck.

But he wasn't worth my time.

I didn't have time to worry about what Liz had said about him or what my father wouldn't.

I wasn't the girl who fell for the hot jerk simply because he had made me feel things I had never felt before. I was smarter than that.

Any experience I had before him didn't feel like that. They had felt like fumbled, sloppy messes compared to Beck. I didn't want to think about how much practice he had to have to be that impactful.

I wasn't an idiot. I knew a guy didn't know how to turn on a girl that well by sitting at home and twiddling his thumbs. And a guy who was that good with his mouth and a simple touch of his hands was not a guy who was also good with hearts.

That was plain and simple.

If I wanted to continue thinking about Beck Clermont, I needed to focus on how to avoid him. I couldn't let thoughts of his cocky smile slip in or the way my heart hammered any time I saw him.

I didn't have time to think about any part of him today. I was here to work, and I couldn't afford to be distracted all day. Not by him or anyone else.

We rounded the corner toward the front desk, and I tightened my ponytail. If I could impress Sam today, then I could possibly get a job in his department in the future. I liked working in the dining room, but Allie had told me that working on the course paid a lot better. And that's all I needed to focus on.

More money, more security.

"Mr. Clermont." My head snapped up as Sam spoke his name, and I quickly peeked around him. Sure enough, the man who owned the club stood there in a blue polo and a pair of khaki shorts.

"Hello, Sam." Mr. Clermont reached out and shook his hand before smiling at me.

"I didn't realize you'd be here today, sir." Sam seemed so nervous around him, and I realized that maybe I should be too. But I couldn't bring myself to. He had been nothing but kind to me since I started and that provided me with a sense of comfort even if it was fake. "Let me just get Josie set up, then I'll get you ready to go."

"We were actually hoping that Josie could be our caddie today."

My heart stopped as I heard Beck's voice. He was leaning against the desk behind his father, and he had the largest smirk on his face when his eyes met mine.

Sam looked between him and his father. "I have several experienced caddies for you, sir. Josie hasn't been trained yet."

"That's okay." Beck pushed off the desk, and I couldn't help but look him over. He wore a pair of black shorts and a bright white polo with a single Nike logo on his chest.

He shouldn't have looked that good. It was what I was used to seeing men in after a round of golf, but it was different with him.

I feared that everything was.

"Who better to give her some on-the-job training?" He was talking to Sam, but he was still looking at me. I knew he was the boss's son, but I still worried about how Sam would react. There was no way in hell he was going to give me a position over here if I was off frolicking with the boss on day one.

"Sam has already asked me to run the reception desk." I avoided looking at Beck, and instead, smiled at his father. "I don't want to leave him stranded."

His father smirked, and it reminded me so much of his son. I wondered if he had been just like him once upon a time. I wondered if that was where Beck's pride came from.

Mr. Clermont was handsome for an older man, and I could imagine him in high school. I imagined him to be exactly like his son.

"Josie, my dad owns this place. You probably shouldn't tell him no."

My gaze jumped to Beck, and I wanted to kill him. "I didn't tell him no. I was telling you no."

I crossed my arms, and his dad chuckled. The sound was warm and kind and made me think maybe he was nothing like his son at all.

"Josie, why don't you join us? It'd be good for Beck to see someone actually working for once."

Beck scoffed, and I couldn't help but smile at that.

I opened my mouth to answer but quickly looked back to Sam. Mr. Clermont may have owned this place, but I had still volunteered to work for Sam, and I wouldn't leave him stranded.

"Go ahead." Sam smiled, but it was tight. "I'll pull one of the other caddies in to cover the desk."

I could feel my cheeks redden and my stomach tighten with anticipation. I had no idea what Beck was doing.

He was here with his father, and I didn't want to be anywhere near him.

I didn't care about what he owned or what kind of power he thought he had.

I didn't want to give him any kind of power over me.

But I didn't have a choice.

Sam handed me a key to a golf cart that I had no idea what to do with, and I followed Mr. Clermont and Beck outside into the crisp morning.

"You ever been golfing, Josie?" Mr. Clermont asked as Beck quickly grabbed his bag of golf clubs before he could.

"I haven't." I wasn't sure what to think of him being so chivalrous, even if it was for his dad. It seemed out of character for him.

"Have you ever driven a golf cart?" He climbed into the passenger seat, and my heart rate spiked. Surely, he didn't actually expect me to drive.

"Never." I held the key out in his direction. "Maybe you should drive."

"No." He shook his head and patted the seat. "It's time you learned. Especially with you working here."

Beck climbed into the back seat that faced backward, but he turned with his arm over the seat and watched me. He was grinning, and the look on his face was enough to make my body remember every single one of his movements from when he had touched me.

From when I had begged him for more.

I climbed into the driver's seat, Beck's arm pressing against my back, and I pushed the key into the ignition. The cart was so quiet I barely even knew it was on, and I had no idea what the hell I was supposed to do next.

Mr. Clermont reached forward and clicked a switch that

said Forward, then I did the only thing I could think of and hit the gas. All three of us jolted forward, and Mr. Clermont shot his hand out to catch himself.

"Shit." I heard Beck swear, and a small laugh bubbled out of my mouth.

"Oh my God. I'm sorry." I was still laughing.

"Do you even have a driver's license?"

"Yes. I have a driver's license," I snapped at Beck's smart-ass question. "I told you I had never driven a golf cart before."

"Help us, Lord." His voice was cut off by his father's.

"Just ease into it." He pointed down at my feet. "The gas pedal is sensitive."

I pressed the pedal again, this time much gentler, and the cart eased forward on the concrete path. There were several other men scattered around claiming a cart, and even a few women. They all waved at Mr. Clermont, who waved at them all with a smile.

I drove past them all, heading toward the course, and I barely even shot us forward when Mr. Clermont pointed to the first hole.

Beck climbed out of the cart and did a move as if he was thanking God. I couldn't help but roll my eyes at him and his dramatics. My driving hadn't been that bad.

He smirked at me, and I couldn't stop smiling.

"Am I supposed to carry your bag or something?" I asked, and Mr. Clermont smiled.

"No. We'll make Beck carry the bags."

Beck rolled his eyes, but he already had a golf bag over each shoulder. They looked heavy, and I knew I probably should have offered to help him, but I didn't. I grinned and walked back to the cart to wait on them.

Mr. Clermont started walking toward the tee box before calling over his shoulder. "Let's go, Josie."

I scrambled to follow him. I didn't realize I would be

needed on the course. I had no earthly idea what the hell I was doing, but I didn't want him to think I was a complete and total idiot. He was the owner, and I would never get moved into any other position if he thought I wasn't capable.

Heck, he probably wouldn't even want me serving food.

Beck stood the bags up next to each other before he pulled a golf club out of one of the bags and handed it to his father.

"This is a driver." His dad was clearly talking to me, but he was looking out to where he was about to hit. "If you're going to work on a golf course, you should at least know the basics."

I watched as Beck stuck something in the ground and placed the ball on top. He made his way back over to where I stood and watched his father. His dad was still talking to me about golf, but I barely heard a thing he said.

Beck's fingers slid against mine. His fingertips ran small circles around mine where they hung between us, the touch tender and far too familiar, and I jerked my hand away before his father could see.

The way Beck grinned at my reaction told me he'd planned on torturing me the entire day. Let's be honest, I had a feeling he planned on torturing me forever.

His dad swung the driver, and the loud whack pulled my attention back to him. He was watching the ball even though I could barely see it, and Beck walked back to the bags to pull out his own golf club. His fingers grazed my lower back as he passed, a touch that was practically undetectable, but I could barely catch my breath.

I watched Beck as he took his turn, not having a single clue where his ball went. I was too busy watching every part of him. The way his shorts hugged his ass, the way his biceps shifted and bunched with his every movement. He was mesmerizing without even trying.

"So, Josie, Jack said you've been doing well in the restaurant.

He said you've quickly become one of the most popular servers."

I jerked my gaze away from Beck's ass to look up at Mr. Clermont.

"Thank you." I smiled, red tainting my cheeks. "I'm really enjoying the job. Everyone has been so nice."

He nodded his head and climbed back into the cart. I attempted to lift his bag to carry to the cart, but it was much heavier than I expected. I tried to put it over my shoulder as I had seen Beck do earlier, but he snatched it out of my hand before I could.

Beck placed both bags on his shoulders, then motioned for me to walk ahead of him. I could feel him staring at me as I walked, and I would be lying if I said there wasn't a part of me that didn't like it.

Beck's attention was dangerous, but it was also thrilling.

And even though I knew I should, a part of me didn't want it to end.

We climbed into the cart, and this time the drive to the next hole was much less eventful. I wouldn't call myself an expert, but I was finally getting the hang of it.

Mr. Clermont didn't speak this time as he grabbed his driver and headed toward his ball. He seemed to be concentrating more than he was earlier. He was doing something. Looking down the line of where he'd swing.

"I'm already winning." Beck grinned as he leaned closer to me. "He's a bit competitive."

"Like father, like son," I murmured.

A few carts passed by us, and each of them seemed glued to whatever he was doing. I knew that he was a powerful man, but they seemed to want to know his every move. They watched him as if they were waiting for him to make a mistake, as if they were waiting for him to fall.

I stepped away from Beck as they passed, not wanting to give them any reason to think anything more.

I didn't need any of these men to think anything of me. I wanted to stay completely off any of their radars.

Beck waited until they passed before he stepped closer to me again. He wasn't allowing me any space.

"Your ass looks really nice in those shorts," he whispered the words against the back of my neck, and his dad could have turned around at any moment to see him. I pushed my elbow into his stomach to get him to back up, but he wasn't having any of it. He pushed harder against me, his front pressing into my back, and the feel of his breath against my skin caused goose bumps to break out over my skin.

"Back up, Beckham," I whispered to him as he ran his nose along the base of my hairline.

"I don't think you want me to." His chest pushed against me as he breathed in and out. The rhythm the same pace as the push and pull of my lungs along with the throbbing between my legs.

His dad was lining up his shot, his attention completely on his golf game, and I knew he couldn't hear Beck's words. But I felt like he was broadcasting them for everyone. It felt like he was screaming, and there was nothing I could do to ignore him.

His dad swung his club, and Beck moved from behind me in a flash. I stumbled back a step, thrown completely off balance by him, and I took a deep breath as he walked toward his father.

I had no idea what the hell I was doing. I was supposed to be working and trying my damnedest to get a position that paid more, but Beck was going to fuck everything up. I would be lucky if they didn't fire me after today.

I didn't feel like I was working. I didn't feel like I was doing anything other than falling farther into Beck's trap.

I moved back toward the cart as Beck and his father spoke,

and I waited by the driver's side for them to finish. I was here to drive them around and do whatever else caddies were supposed to do. What I wasn't here to do was let Beck touch me and push me to the point where I would beg him for more.

Because I knew I would.

My body was so tense that I felt like I could snap at any moment.

We went through the next few holes in the same manner. I stood by the cart while the two of them golfed. Beck kept his eyes on me as he did. Every move I made was tracked by him. Every breath I took was affected by his gaze.

He looked like he wanted to say something to me, to touch me, to make me feel like I was crawling out of my skin.

But I didn't give him the opportunity. I was avoiding him. I smiled at his father and made small talk, but I avoided looking at Beck at all costs. It didn't matter that he tapped his fingers against the side of my neck as I drove, or that he toyed with my ponytail as his father pointed something out on the property.

I refused to let him know how much every single touch was affecting me.

We were around the tenth hole when another cart pulled up directly behind us. I glanced behind me before turning forward, but then I spun back to face the cart behind me.

My father sat beside a boy who was wearing a matching outfit to me, and someone I didn't know rode in the back. I climbed out of the cart and walked toward my father.

He shot a tight smile just as Mr. Clermont reached him and shook his hand.

"How are you, Joseph?"

"I'm doing well. Any day I get to golf is a good day."

Mr. Clermont laughed, but Beck didn't so much as smile. He stood behind his father, and he looked like he had about a million things on his mind that he wanted to say.

He looked at my father like he had looked at Lucas. His eyes narrowed, his nostrils slightly flared, and his rage barely in check. He clearly hated the men of my family, and even though I already knew that, it felt a bit shocking to see the way he was reacting to my dad.

"I see you managed to get my daughter out here." My father looked over at me as his caddie carried his bag over to the grass.

"She's been a great help so far," Mr. Clermont lied. I had barely done more than almost throw him from the cart.

"I didn't even realize you worked today," he said it like he knew my schedule any other day. He may have been my father, but I had seen him as much since I'd been living with him as I did before. He was still an absent father, even with me living under his roof.

Regardless of how he wanted to act.

"Here I am." I shrugged and looked back toward Beck. He was no longer watching my father. His gaze was directly on me, and the playfulness from before had slipped from every inch of his face.

"Beckham, are you ready for your senior year?"

I winced when I heard my father address Beck. I didn't even know why Beck hated him so much, but I knew with certainty that he did.

"As ready as I'll ever be." He stared at my father as he spoke, and I held my breath. Beck didn't seem like the kind of guy that ever held back.

But he did.

He stared at my father, and he kept his mouth shut in a thin line.

If my father could feel the tension, he didn't so much as blink. He acted like he was talking to his closest friends and had no concern for anything.

But my father was rarely concerned with much. If it didn't directly affect his wallet, he didn't care.

"Well, we'll let you get back to your game." My father smiled before looking at me. "You have a second?"

I nodded and stepped behind him as he walked away from the rest of the group. He stopped when we were out of earshot, and his gaze slid over my outfit.

"I thought you were working in the dining room."

"I am." I straightened out my polo. "I volunteered to pick up a shift on the course today."

"If you need money, I have plenty."

I didn't answer him because he knew how I felt about that. I didn't want any of his money. Not what I could avoid.

He was already putting a roof over my head and food in my belly. I hated that thought alone. If I had a way that I could completely provide for myself, I would. If I could go home to my mom's house and live on my own, I would do it in a heartbeat.

But he had all the control.

When I didn't answer, he huffed and moved on. "Don't forget that school starts tomorrow. You need to get home tonight and get ready for your first day."

"I'll be there." I was always there. With the exception of the couple times I had gone out with Allie, I always left work and went straight home.

He looked out to where Mr. Clermont and Beck stood by the cart, and he looked like he was hesitant to say what he said next. Which was odd because he never hesitated about anything.

He was sure and firm, and he never let his assurance waver.

"Beck Clermont isn't a good influence." He nodded his head toward them, but I didn't look. "I'd rather you didn't spend your time with him."

I bit down on my tongue until I couldn't stand the pain. He didn't really get to tell me who was a good influence.

He was a man who had chosen not to take care of his own

child because he refused to give up his lifestyle and my mother refused to stay with a man who valued money and power above his family.

"As you've already told me."

"Then you should listen," he snapped, and my spine straightened.

If I wanted to be around Beck, I would. My father's opinion of him wouldn't sway me one way or another.

That was a lie. It made me want to be around him more. If Beck Clermont pissed off my father, then I would gladly spend time with him for that reason alone.

I stared up at my father as he adjusted the golf glove on his hand. "I know the two of us don't exactly see eye to eye on most things, but this isn't up for discussion."

I bit down on my lip and didn't say a word. He didn't care what I had to say.

Beck lifted his chin as soon as I walked away from my father and climbed back into the cart, silently asking me if I was okay.

I gave him a single nod and planted a smile on my face before driving us to the next hole.

Beck was far less playful as the rest of their game continued. He concentrated on his game, and much less on me. I knew his mood was off the moment he saw my father, but I would be lying if I said it didn't hurt me in some way.

Whatever Beck thought of me, he couldn't separate me from my family. He may have let himself forget for a moment, so had I, but all either of us needed was a reminder.

But I wanted Beck Clermont regardless of our circumstances. I wanted him regardless of what his plans were for me, and I didn't know if anything could change that. Because the reality was he wanted me, and he was bringing out the version of myself I'd been wanting to be since I moved here. He might be doing it in the worst way possible, but I couldn't deny it. I just needed him to see me as Josie, the new girl in town, the new girl who shared the same name as his worst enemy.

I pulled the cart back up to the clubhouse, and there were many more people there now than there were when we left. Mr. Clermont climbed out of the cart and was immediately bombarded by people talking to him.

I watched Beck as he carried his and his father's bags over to another guy who quickly grabbed them, and I couldn't stop watching him as some girl who also wore a Clermont Bay Country Club uniform spoke to him.

I had no reason to be jealous. Beck owned this place, and this girl was clearly an employee, but she didn't look like she was discussing business. She looked like her talk was anything but professional.

Not that I could talk. I was at work and I had let him be far too close to me to ever be considered acceptable.

I was sure it was the way Beck worked, all a part of his game, and as she leaned forward and whispered something in his ear, I couldn't stand there and watch him do it.

I went through the front door and saw some guy at the front desk who looked overwhelmed. I walked behind the desk and tried to help him as best I could without a lick of training. He handed me a few keys to hand out to members and had me call the bar for a few orders that needed to be taken to carts.

I did everything he said, and I tried to work hard enough to fight the urge to look back out the front windows at Beck.

It didn't matter if he was still with that girl. It also didn't matter that I was bothered by that simple fact when he had been driving me crazy since the moment I met him.

School was starting tomorrow, and I was going to have to face it during every part of the day.

I set a cooler of craft beer on the back of one of the carts and a man with more gray hair than not thanked me.

Beck looked my way as I passed him, but I didn't stop. I just continued to do my job and pretend like he wasn't there. I tried to pretend like he hadn't flipped a switch the moment he saw my father.

Sam was standing behind the desk when I returned. "What else can I do?"

I didn't want him to think I was horrible at my job, even if I may have not made the best first impression.

"Can you head over to the bar? They need some more ice."

"Of course." That was something I could do. I had to fill the ice all the time in the dining room.

I checked my phone as I walked toward the bar that was connected to the course for easy access and saw a message from Allie.

I wish you weren't working today. We could be shopping.

I wish I wasn't either.

I had turned Allie down originally to go shopping. She needed school clothes and I didn't. She would be able to dress normally, and I would be in some uptight uniform.

I should have gone. If I had gone, I wouldn't be here, and I wouldn't have seen Beck. I hadn't told Allie about what happened with him outside of his father's office, and I wasn't sure if I would.

I grabbed the ice bucket and headed to the back of this wing of the building where the ice machine was kept. I was surprised by how big the grounds were. Of course, you could see the building was massive from outside, but once you were inside, it felt like a maze. The dining room and a few meeting rooms were at the center of the club. The golf course along with a gym, sauna, and pool were to the left, and I didn't have a clue what was on the right. The farthest I had been that way was to Mr. Clermont's office.

I hadn't dared venture around without a chaperone. Not without Allie.

Today was the first time I had even been near the course.

The large metal scoop was heavy in my hand as I flipped open the lid to the ice machine. I needed to focus on work. Work, school, and getting out of here.

All three things would be vital to my success.

I needed the money, I needed my dad to give me what was rightfully mine, and I needed to get the hell away from this place.

The door to the machine slammed shut, and I jumped.

Beck was standing there, and I hadn't even heard him. I was so lost in my head that I wasn't paying attention.

"You scared me." I dropped the scoop in the ice bucket and took a small step back.

He looked pissed off. He had no right to be, but it was written all over his face.

"What are you doing?" His hazel eyes looked almost black, and even though that should have put some fear in me, I found nothing but an ache low in my belly.

I looked down at the ice bucket and back at him. "Getting ice."

"Don't be a smart-ass."

"I didn't realize I was."

"Why did you run off?"

"I didn't run off." I flipped the ice machine door back open and grabbed another scoop full. "I'm working. You know, work?"

He looked like he wanted to pummel me, but I kept going. "Some of us have to do that for a living."

"Don't play poor girl with me, Josie. I know who your daddy is."

"I don't live off my daddy." I shoved the scoop back into the ice harder than I needed to. "What's that like?"

"You don't know shit about me." His lips were stretched tight and his chest puffed in anger.

"And you don't know shit about me."

He stepped toward me, but I held my ground. I wouldn't dare let him see that he intimidated me. Even if I could barely control the way my hands trembled.

His chest hit mine, and I let the ice scoop fall from my hand as I stared up at him. His chest heaved, pressing against mine with a force that did little to calm my own temper, but he didn't say anything.

He just stared at me with a look on his face that was completely unreadable. He was angry, sure, but there was something else.

There was something he wanted to say that he wouldn't. There was something that he was hiding.

"You should go." I looked toward the door where he must have come in through, the same door that was still standing wide open. Anyone could walk in here and see him pressed against me.

"I think you should probably not tell me what I should be doing." He touched my throat with gentle fingers that were in complete contrast to the rage in his eyes. I knew that he had no intentions of walking away from me right now. He didn't care if he was putting my job at risk. He didn't care about anything but himself.

"You hate my family," I reminded him, and his eyes flicked from my throat where he was watching his hand on me.

"Trust me. I'm aware of the fact."

I could have sworn his hand spasmed around my neck as if he wanted to press harder, as if the thought of me being one of them was going to cause him to lose control.

"Why?"

His gaze lowered to my mouth before moving back to my eyes. "Because they're trash."

That didn't tell me anything. It didn't tell me what happened between them.

"And you hate me?" I whispered because I didn't want it to be true.

He didn't answer me though. Instead, he smashed his mouth against mine, and his teeth felt like they would draw blood against my lips.

He wasn't gentle or smooth. He was kissing me like he was trying to prove something, maybe to himself, maybe to me. I wasn't sure.

But I knew that I didn't want it to stop.

Even though he couldn't even say that he didn't hate me, and in that moment, I hated him, I still wanted him more than I had ever wanted anything before in my life.

But I couldn't just let him have whatever he wanted.

I pushed against his chest and forced his mouth away from mine.

"That's not good enough." I shook my head and tried to clear the fog of lust.

He leaned forward as if to ignore me, but I turned my face before he could kiss me again. If he did, I knew that I wouldn't stop him.

"I know you two were friends. What happened?"

Beck leaned back slightly and stared down at me as his chest rose and fell against mine. "We were friends."

"And?" My pulse raced, and I could feel his beating as fast as mine under his shirt.

"And he touched things that didn't belong to him."

What?

"So this is about a girl?" I pushed harder against him, but he didn't budge. He didn't move an inch, and he didn't say anything more.

"So this is just some sort of revenge on Lucas?" I pointed between the two of us. "He fucked something of yours so you're going to fuck something of his?"

He was absolutely insane.

I moved, trying to push past him, but he pushed his body harder against me, trapping me beneath him.

"You are not his." His voice was sharp and full of venom that it made me want to believe what he said.

"Then whose am I?" I challenged him. I was so tired of his bullshit answers and his fucked-up game. I just wanted to know what he wanted.

I needed to know what he was thinking.

His hand moved back up my neck as he stared down at me. He was so fucking hesitant to say what he said next, but his words rocked me to my core.

"You're mine."

His hand on my throat tightened as he slammed his mouth down on mine. I met him with just as much force as I tried to hold on to what he had just said.

His opposite hand gripped my thigh, and I didn't hesitate as I lifted it around his waist. The movement gave him an opening, and he took it. He pressed into me, his center hitting mine, and I moaned into his mouth at the sensation.

His lack of gentleness with his mouth was even more severe with his hips. He was brutal as he pushed against me over and over, his hips setting a rhythm my heart couldn't seem to keep up with. I had never been touched like this before, I had never felt such need, but I knew that I didn't want it to stop.

"Beck," I said his name, but I didn't know what I was asking for. His name felt like more. It felt like I was asking him to give me everything when I should have been asking for nothing at all.

This boy was no good for me. He was toxic. We both knew it, but that didn't stop me from grinding my hips against his or allowing him to lift my other leg and wrap it around his hips. I was pinned to the ice machine, his body fully in control of both of us, and he was still kissing my mouth as if he had never tasted something so addicting.

His hands were resting on my hips, and I wanted them to move. I wanted him to touch me everywhere. I could feel him over every part of me, but none of it was enough.

The smell of his cologne surrounded me, and his skin was hot against mine. I felt like I was burning from the inside out.

He pulled his mouth away from mine, and he looked down at me with a ragged breath. He was warring with himself, that much was easy to see. I didn't know if he was at war over how far he wanted to take this or if he was battling with himself over what he had just said.

But that hesitation was there.

His mouth had felt brutal, his hips sure, but I knew that he was still holding himself back from me. I had no idea what I wanted from Beck, but I knew one thing for sure.

I didn't want him to hold back. Not right now. Not when my body was begging him for more.

I rolled my hips against him as he stared at me, and I saw the pleasure flick across his face. He leaned back, leaving my back pressed against the hard metal, and he stared down at where our hips connected.

For a moment, embarrassment rushed through me. I had no idea what I was doing. I wasn't even sure if the way I moved felt half as good to him as it did me. I stopped the movement of my hips, waiting for him to say something, but his hand immediately dropped to my ass and forced me to move again.

"Don't stop moving, Josie." He was still watching our centers, but I didn't care.

I wanted him to want me as much as I wanted him.

I moved against him as he watched, and I hadn't realized how turned on I would be by that simple act. Beck was watching me, and I suddenly felt like I was where life began and ended for him. I usually felt like I was the one orbiting around him. He had felt like he was the center of gravity ever since I arrived in Clermont Bay. He pulled me in, and he refused to let go.

But right now, everything felt different. He felt like the one who couldn't stop. He felt like the one who could no longer stay away.

It felt like a dangerous push and pull, a game that would have no good ending, but I was still dying to play it.

"Beck," I said his name again because there was a tightness building in my belly with so much pleasure that I was sure I would die if he didn't do something.

His gaze snapped up to mine as his name passed my lips, and as his deep hazel eyes met mine, it was like he had finally made a decision. The hesitation in his eyes had all but disappeared.

He kept one hand planted on my ass, forcing me against him, as his other moved to my breast. It was rough, and I gasped as he squeezed my nipple between his thumb and fore-finger. He swallowed the sound as his mouth found mine again. His teeth bit down on my bottom lip before he sucked it into his mouth, and I swear I felt the movement straight to my core.

I ground harder against him, desperate for more friction, and I gasped as Beck suddenly dropped me back to my feet.

Disappointment overwhelmed me, and I pushed my hair out of my face. Here I was riding his hips, begging for more, and he dropped me down as if he wasn't affected at all.

I looked up at him, embarrassed by how I had just acted, but I didn't get a chance to see his face. He spun me around, his hands forcing my hips around, and my hands pressed into the ice machine as he pressed into me.

"I'm not done with you." His voice was directly at my ear just before he bit down on my earlobe, and I jolted forward, my breasts hitting the metal.

His hand snaked around my body and pressed into my stomach. I was certain he could feel it flutter beneath his touch, but he didn't give me time to second-guess what was happening. He used his opposite hand to grip my chin and he turned my mouth to his.

He kissed me just as he pushed his hand down the front of my shorts. My heart hammered in my chest, and I kissed him with everything I had. His fingers slid against my pussy, and I couldn't concentrate on anything but that feeling and trying not to freak out.

"God, you're so wet." He groaned as his fingers started to move with more determination. He pressed against my clit, and my hips shot forward.

There wasn't a single part of me that wanted him to stop. My hips were practically chasing the movement of his hand even though I was pinned beneath him.

I could feel his erection pressing into my ass, and I swallowed as I ground my ass against him.

His deep groan only spurred me on, and it felt like I was being pulled in a million different directions. I was chasing my pleasure through his hand in front of me and his pleasure behind me. I felt like I was chasing my own heartbeat, my breathing, my thoughts.

Everything was getting away from me, just out of my grasp, but I chased it still.

Beck pushed a finger inside of me, and I bit my lip to keep myself from making too much noise. He pumped in and out of me as his thumb strummed against my clit.

It was all too much, too fast, and I felt like I was drowning.

I kissed him like he was my only source of air. Like my mere existence depended on the way he touched me.

And part of me feared that it did. I feared that I would never feel anything like this again.

"Oh, God," I cried against his mouth, but he didn't waver. His hand only seemed to speed up and move in a way that felt like he was going to ruin me.

My stomach tightened to the point of pain, and I was about to ask him to stop when he pushed his thumb down against my clit, harder than before.

The change of sensation threw me over the edge, and I moaned so loudly that Beck gently shushed me as he brought me down. I sagged against him, my body completely spent, and I watched as he pulled his hand from my pants and slipped his wet fingers into his mouth.

I was too exhausted to look away or to feel embarrassed. His eyes stared into mine, and he moaned around his fingers, and the only thought I had was that I somehow still wanted more.

The insanity wasn't lost on me. He had just given me more pleasure than I had ever felt in my life, but I didn't want it to stop. If anything, it only made me crave him more. It made me feel like I was mad.

"Shit." Beck pushed away from me quickly and snapped open the ice machine door. I barely had enough time to even look up before he grabbed the bucket and started filling it with ice. I didn't understand what he was doing until Sam pushed through the door.

The door that had been left open. The door that we could have easily been caught through.

I was such a freaking idiot.

Sam looked from Beck to me, then back again, and I knew that he knew something was going on. If he couldn't tell just from looking at us, I knew that he could hear my thundering heart from across the room.

"What's going on in here?" His voice boomed, and I startled at the sound.

"I don't know, Sam," Beck spoke before I could even think of a simple word. "Maybe you should show your new employees where things are before you send them off in search of things."

Sam's face fell the slightest bit and he looked like he had been reprimanded by the boss, and for a moment, I forgot that he had. I hadn't just been caught fucking around at work. I had been caught with the owner's son.

"I'm sorry, Josie. I didn't realize you didn't know."

"It's okay." I forced a smile and gave Beck a look, telling him to calm down. "I've just never been to this side of the club before."

It wasn't a complete lie. I hadn't, but I didn't need Beck's help finding the ice machine.

"Beck, if you want to get back, I can finish helping Josie."

Beck lifted the scoop out of the ice again and finished filling the bucket. He handed the scoop to me as he grabbed the bucket in his hands. He looked like he wanted to say something but thought better of it. Instead, he pushed the bucket into Sam's hand, then waved him toward the door.

Sam looked between us again, and I knew that he didn't believe a word we had said. He didn't have any proof, but he had doubt and that was bad enough. That was enough to make him never hire me in his department.

I followed after Sam as he pushed out the door, but Beck grabbed my hand. I shook my hand from his and took another step. Sam was already on the other side of the door and couldn't see us, but I didn't care.

I had already risked enough today. The last thing I needed was to be fired because I was an idiot who just needed one more touch. Beck didn't share the same concerns.

He walked up behind me, forcing me to a stop with his hands on my hips, and pressed a gentle kiss to my neck.

"This isn't over," he whispered, but I didn't reply. I pushed out the door before I made any more bad decisions when it came to him.

Because I knew he was a bad decision. Every part of him. It didn't matter that I wanted him and had to force my feet to move me forward and away from him. He was a terrible idea.

I knew that.

But I didn't care.

I looked over my shoulder and smiled at him. He was a terrible decision that I knew I would choose again.

I didn't have a choice really. He smiled back at me, his smirk promising more, and I knew that I couldn't just walk away from him.

I was only here for one year, then I would walk away from it all.

I would leave Beck, my father, all of it.

I wouldn't leave a trace of me behind.

CHAPTER THIRTEEN

JOSIE

I didn't want to be here.

This school was nothing like the school I went to back home, and even though I didn't want to, I couldn't help searching the front of the school for Beck.

We hadn't talked about school at all with one another, and I had no idea how to act around him here. I had no idea how he would act.

Especially after yesterday.

I wasn't foolish to think that it had meant anything to him more than what it was. That was fine.

But I still couldn't get his words out of my head.

You're mine.

I hadn't seen him at all yesterday after what happened. I put my head down and worked hard as Sam watched me. I knew that he was waiting for me to mess up. I could tell by the way he surveyed my every move.

But I gave him no reason.

Whatever he thought he saw in the room with the ice machine was just that. Thoughts. After that, I didn't give him reason to suspect a thing. I did what I had intended to do when I volunteered for the shift. I worked my ass off.

And I thought about Beck the entire time.

I knew no one here. Lucas had to be here early for baseball workouts, and even though the two of us had felt awkward since the morning he came home drunk, I wished he was with me.

"You look lost." I looked over at the blonde as she let a small puff of smoke pass her lips. "You new here?"

I gripped the straps of my backpack and looked her over. She wore the same uniform as I did, one that was required of all students at Clermont Bay Prep, but she looked so much better in it. Her body filled out the uniform far better than mine, and her skirt somehow fell on a far more attractive spot on her thighs.

"It's that noticeable?"

"Yes." She pressed the cherry of her joint into the brick before grabbing a bag off the ground. "Plus, most of us have been in school together since we were babies."

"Yay." My voice sounded just as thrilled as I felt.

"Don't worry. It's not that bad." She nodded for me to follow her as she started walking toward the school.

"What's your name?" she asked without even turning to see if I was behind her.

"Josie. You?"

"Cami." She pulled open the heavy double doors and strode into the hallway as if this place didn't intimidate her at all. I guess if I was her, I wouldn't be intimidated either.

"You like to party?"

"Yes?" My answer was hesitant, and of course, she picked up on it.

"That sounded like a no." She laughed and ran her gaze from my head to my toes, and I knew she was sizing me up. She was trying to determine exactly where I fit in here, and so was I. "We're having a party at my house this weekend."

"What about your parents?" I followed her down the hallway as I stared down at my schedule to find my first class.

"They'll be out of town." She said it like it didn't matter one way or another to her. "Where's your first class?"

"Mr. Fouch, English, room 201." I read the first line of my schedule.

"Same as me." She linked her arm in mine, and even though I didn't know a single thing about this girl, I was happy to have someone by my side as I walked to my first class. Even if she was a complete stranger.

I sat at the desk beside her, and I pulled a blank notebook out of my backpack as I waited for the teacher to start. It was weird seeing all the students in matching uniforms, but somehow looking so different at the same time.

I had never had to wear a uniform before. Never even seen a school that had to, but I still pulled it on this morning like I knew what I was doing. Like I knew what the hell I was getting into.

The students were all looking at me as if they hadn't seen a new student in their entire lives. It was everyone's first day back, but they didn't seem to care about each other.

They were too interested in me.

"Good morning, everyone." I pulled my attention to the teacher and watched as he adjusted his tie. He looked like he was already stressed out, but it was only the first day of the school year. "I'm going to complete a roll call. Please say here when I call your name."

He went through the list of names and everyone responded with a bored 'here' as if they couldn't be bothered. For such an elite school, the students didn't seem to care.

"Josephine Vos." I winced as my name passed his lips.

"Here." Several eyes turned back in my direction, but I avoided them all. Except for Cami, who shot her leg out and kicked the edge of my chair.

I looked over at her and her mouth was practically gaping. "What?" I whispered because Mr. Fouch was still taking roll.

"You're Joseph Vos's daughter?" She said it like it was supposed to mean something more than it did. She said it like he wasn't the worst father in the world.

"Unfortunately."

She chuckled before covering her mouth with her hand. "Holy shit. I didn't even realize he had any other kids."

Other.

Because Lucas had been his only one.

I guess he belonged to him more than I did.

"Long-lost." I looked back up at our teacher and hoped she'd catch my drift that I didn't want to talk about my father. I didn't want to think about him at all.

"I bet Lucas is having a field day with you."

I hated the way she said that. I hated that she even knew him, but of course, she did. They all did. I was the outsider here.

I tried to ignore Cami for the rest of the class, but she was back on me as soon as the bell rang. Apparently, my last name had made me far more interesting than I had been before she knew it.

A name I hated would determine where I stood with these people. It would tell them everything they needed to know about me. Every single thing that they cared to know.

But I didn't care.

One school year. That was all I had to make it through.

The opinions of these people didn't matter. They would go on with their charmed lives, and I would be gone.

They wouldn't even remember that I was here, and I would make sure that I forgot every single one of them.

Even Beck.

I would make sure I forgot him just like the rest.

"Walk with me." She slid her arm in mine, no longer oblivious over whether I was following her or not, and I tried to calm my heart.

People were staring at us as I walked with her, and I knew it wouldn't be long before every damn one of them knew my name. They would all have figured out who I was without ever saying a word to me.

The halls were crowded with people all wearing the same uniform as me, but they were still so easy to tell apart. The cliques of every other high school still present through the money and privilege.

But none of them looked like him.

I spotted him before he ever noticed me. Beck was leaning against a locker, his back to us, but I knew it was him. His uniform jacket hung from his arm, the sleeves of his shirt pushed up to the elbow, and I hated that he looked so good. Even though I couldn't see his face, he still demanded my attention.

Cami let go of my arm just as we reached where he stood, and I prayed she would just keep walking by. Avoiding him was the only plan I had at the moment. I didn't know how else to deal with him. Not here.

But Cami had no intentions of walking past the king of Clermont Bay. I tightened my hands on the straps of my backpack as she pressed her body into his back and wrapped her arms around his shoulders.

He smiled over his shoulder at her, and I knew, I knew deep in my gut it was a smile he didn't give anyone else. That was a smile he reserved only for her, and I felt like I was going to be sick.

She pushed to the tips of her toes, and I couldn't stop myself from watching as she pushed her lips toward his. Beck Clermont meant nothing to me. Not a damn thing, but I could still barely breathe.

He had touched me. His body convincing mine that I wanted him without any damn effort on his part, and he had her.

Of course, he had her.

He was Beck fucking Clermont.

He turned his head at the last second before their mouths touched, and her lips pressed against the corner of his as his gaze met mine. There was a moment of shock, but I didn't know what he had to be shocked about. I was the fool.

I knew from the moment I had met Beck that he was cruel, but I would have expected him to tell me about her.

I had no idea why.

He hadn't cared about me from the moment I met him.

I schooled my expression, and I prayed that he didn't see an ounce of my being affected on my face.

I refused to allow him to think I was affected when he was touching her. When she was touching him. *God, she was still touching him.*

She dropped back to her feet, and she looked back in my direction with a smile on her face. "Have you all met my new friend, Josie?"

"Hey, Josie." Olly smiled at me from where he leaned against the locker next to Beck. He looked back and forth between me and where Beck and Cami still stood together. Did he know? Did Beck tell him what I had let him do?

"Hi." I tucked my hair behind my ear and looked down the hallway for some sort of escape. Any excuse to get away.

"You're not going to say hi to me?" My gaze snapped up to Beck as he spoke. He had a smile on his face, and I noticed that Cami was still clinging to his arm even though he wasn't touching her. Of course, I noticed.

"Hello, Beckham."

He grinned harder as one of the guys beside him chuckled. I didn't know if it was Olly or Carson or someone I didn't know. I didn't care.

"You two know each other?" Cami looked between the two of us, and I felt bad for her. I didn't know the extent of her and Beck's relationship, but it was clear that she had walked in here today expecting one.

I had no such expectations, but I had assumed that there was no one else. That was my foolish mistake, and one I wasn't willing to make again.

"Josie and I go way back." Beck was laying it on thick, and everyone around him seemed to hang on to his every word. It didn't matter that he wasn't saying a single bit of truth. He was important, and that was all that mattered.

"We don't." I tightened my hands around my strap and pulled out my schedule. I needed to find my next class. I didn't have time to worry about him.

"We most certainly do."

I looked up at him and crinkled the paper in my hand. "I work for Beck's father at the country club." I didn't say anything more because there was nothing else to say.

Nothing else mattered.

"Ouch." He rubbed his hand over his chest before snatching my paper out of my hand. "Where's your next class, Vos?"

Those around us who hadn't already known my name were now looking at me more intensely than a moment before, and I hated it.

"Give me my schedule back, Beckham."

There were a few chuckles, and Cami leaned farther into his side. "He goes by Beck."

"Oh." I pretended like I hadn't known. "I'm sorry, Beck. I hadn't realized."

He grinned as he read over my paper but didn't respond. I was trying to get under his skin, but that was impossible. Beck Clermont was impenetrable.

"It looks like your next class is with me." He tucked my schedule in his pocket and started moving down the hall. He didn't say a word to anyone else. Not even a goodbye to Cami.

She didn't look happy about it either. But I didn't have time to worry about that, I was too busy trying to catch up to Beck so I could get my schedule back and find my next class.

Everyone was watching as I jogged behind him to catch up. "Give me my schedule, Beck."

"Oh. Now I'm Beck?"

"Just give me my schedule." I held out my hand, but he made no move to give it to me. He liked having me at his mercy, and he wasn't going to do anything that took away his advantage.

"Are you having a good first day?" I felt like I was getting

whiplash. Was he seriously just asking me about my day after I
had just seen him with her?

"Oh, yes. I'm having an amazing time." My sarcasm was
clear.

"Yeah?" He chuckled softly as he walked. "First period was
good?"

"Oh yeah." I nodded and stepped around a guy who was
picking up his books off the floor. "I made a new friend who
invited me to her party this weekend. I think you know her." I
tapped my chin as he watched me. "You know? Your girlfriend."

"She's not my girlfriend," he said it so casually that I
couldn't stop myself from looking up at him.

"She looked like your girlfriend."

"And you look jealous." He stopped by the classroom door
and students stared at us as they walked past.

"I am not jealous."

"You sure?" he asked as he raised his hand and pushed
some hair behind my ear.

I wanted to slap that hand away, but I didn't want to cause a
bigger scene. I didn't need to give these people any other reason
to think, talk, or look at me.

I wanted to be under the radar. Off of it completely.

But standing here arguing with their king wasn't going to
accomplish that. It was only going to make everything worse.

But I couldn't just walk away and let him think that I was
jealous. I was, insanely so, but he didn't need to know that. He
didn't need to know that yesterday had meant anything to me.

If he wanted to treat it as nothing, then so would I.

"I'm positive." I brushed past him and walked into class.

I moved to one of the seats at the back of the class. I didn't
even care that he still had my schedule. I would be late for my
next class and go to the office to get one printed. They wouldn't
fault me on my first day.

Beck plopped down into the desk in front of me and smiled

at me over his shoulder. He was perfectly in my line of sight when I would be looking at the teacher, and he knew it. Beck didn't do anything without a plan.

I stared forward, trying my hardest to ignore him, and I listened to the teacher as she spoke. This was calculus, and I needed to pay attention. I didn't have time to deal with Beck in this class.

I wouldn't let him distract me.

He had a notebook in front of him, but I didn't see him take a single note as she spoke.

My phone buzzed in my bag on the floor, and I quickly grabbed it before she could hear it. She had just gone over her class rules, and no phones were at the top of the list.

I wasn't trying to get in trouble during the first day.

I pressed my phone between my knees so the buzzing wouldn't be heard, and when it went off two more times, I quickly checked it.

You were jealous.

But you have nothing to be jealous of.

Me and Cami just have a history.

I clicked the screen off without replying. I didn't care about his and Cami's history. That was a lie, I absolutely cared, but I didn't want him to know that.

As far as he was concerned, nothing about him mattered to me. Not who he was with in the past or present because I was no longer going to be a part of that equation.

My phone buzzed again, and the urge to quickly check it was so overwhelming. Even if I didn't want him to know, I desperately wanted to know what he had to say.

The urge felt irrational and obsessive, and I tried my hardest not to give in to it.

But I failed.

I tapped the screen of my phone and there his name was again. I had saved him as Clermont in my phone, and I knew that he would probably hate that. I smiled as I read his next message.

Trust me.

Trust him. He wanted me to trust him? I couldn't think of anything more preposterous. Beck was the definition of untrustworthy. He was the most treacherous boy I had ever met, and I couldn't be foolish enough to trust him. Even if I desperately wanted to.

After what you said to your father? You want me to trust you?

I tucked the phone under my thigh, and I refused to look at it again.

I could feel him regularly looking over his shoulder to look at me, but I didn't acknowledge him. If I was going to make it through this class, through this school year, then I had to stick to my original plan.

Put my head down, work my ass off, and forget about him.

That last part was relatively new, but it was the most important. Beck would do nothing but make this year more difficult.

The bell rang, and I shoved my notebook into my bag. I had every intention of walking right by him when I stood, but he threw out his long legs and blocked my path as the other students filtered out of the room.

"I was angry when you overheard me and my father." He had my schedule in his hand, and he rested it against his stomach. He looked completely at ease.

"I don't care, Beck." I shook my head and tried to step over his legs.

"You're a bad liar." He leaned forward, and he tugged on the bottom edge of my skirt to bring me closer to him. "But you look so hot in this uniform."

"Does it remind you of your girlfriend?" I cocked my head to the side, and even though he was amused, I saw the edge of annoyance in his gaze. He wasn't used to being pushed so hard.

I was sure of it. I was sure that Cami rolled over and let him have anything he wanted.

"It reminds me that you're trouble." He tugged harder, and I was forced to take a step forward. "I told you that she's not my girlfriend."

"And I don't believe you." I looked down at him, and there was something about it that made me feel braver. Him looking up at me like that, it gave me a sense of false control. "Cami's probably waiting for you." I nodded toward the door.

Everyone else was already gone from the class, even the teacher, but the door was wide open and there were plenty of students walking by.

"But I'm talking to you." He fingered the edge of my skirt, and I knew I should have slapped his hand away. It made absolutely zero sense that I didn't, but nothing was making sense.

I pressed my knees together as his finger moved, and I remembered what his hands had felt like yesterday.

"Do you need a reminder of what happened yesterday?" His finger dropped from my skirt and ran a trail over my bare skin until he met my knee-high socks.

I stared down at him, and the first word on my lips should have been no. I should have shouted it at him so he could get it through his thick skull, but that word never came.

His hand wrapped around the back of my knee, and I felt a mix of fear and anticipation over what he would do next. He smelled so good, his dark cologne overwhelming me and making me make stupid decisions.

"Do I need to eat this pussy to remind you who it belongs to?"

My stomach tightened at his filthy words. No one had ever spoken to me like that, let alone touch me in that way. I couldn't concentrate on what I should have said at that moment. All I could think about was the way he used his wicked tongue and what it would feel like there.

I could feel myself getting wet, and I knew that he knew it as well. He knew that he was turning me on. It was his intent, and he had hit it with minimal effort.

"Beck." I took the smallest step toward him and his pupils dilated. They became so large his eyes almost appeared black, and I glanced down to see if he was as turned on as I was. His erection was straining against his pants, and there was an overwhelming part of me that wanted to explore his body.

"Yesterday was a mistake." I slapped his hand away from my leg. "I don't think your girlfriend would like that."

I wanted to know what every inch of him looked like beneath his facade. I wanted to know what every inch tasted like. I wanted to have as much control over him as he had over me.

"Mr. Clermont, do you need a map to find your way out of my classroom?"

I jumped back, our teacher's voice startling me, and Beck's hand fell from my skin.

"No, ma'am." He stood, grabbing his bag, and his body pressed against mine for the slightest moment before he turned to face her. "I was just helping Ms. Vos figure out the rest of her schedule."

She didn't believe a word of his bullshit. "Then let's make sure she gets there on time. Shall we?"

He nodded and reached for my hand, and for some stupid reason, I didn't pull it away.

CHAPTER FOURTEEN

Everybody was talking about her. More importantly, they were talking about me with her, and I was eating that shit up.

I had barely seen her since our second-period class. I didn't know if it was due to her avoiding me or if her first day was actually keeping her busy, but by the time I hit the locker room after class for practice, I had the overwhelming urge to go find her.

How was the rest of your first day? I text her before setting my phone in my locker and pulling off my shirt. I hated wearing this damn uniform. It was so damn stuffy and pretentious, and I planned to burn them all the moment I graduated from this place.

The rest of the baseball team was pouring into the locker room, and Olly threw his bag down beside mine as he plopped down on the bench.

"Well, you made quite the stir today."

"Whatever do you mean?" I kicked off my shoes and undid my belt.

"Cami's pissed." He raised his eyebrows like I should have been scared, but I didn't care. Cami had more shit to worry about than me. She wasn't going to lose her queen bee status suddenly because I was interested in another girl.

She had been at the top since we were in middle school, and nobody fell from the top that easily. Not without reason.

And Josie mattered more than Cami's reputation.

Frankie mattered more.

I couldn't lie and say I wasn't enjoying what was happening between Josie and me. I hadn't expected her to be so fiery and so brazen. She didn't give a shit that I was a Clermont, even though she liked to remind me of that fact often.

It was refreshing and arousing.

When I touched Josie, she was only being touched by me. Not my last name or my family's money. And, God, when I touched her. It was unlike anything I had ever experienced before.

She was so reactive to my touch. Her body so responsive.

If I didn't know any better, I would say that she had barely ever been touched before. But Josie didn't hold the same hesitancy as a girl who had never been touched. She was too bold for that. Too eager.

She was a girl who knew what she wanted, even if she didn't want to.

She wanted me regardless, and I sure as fuck wanted her.

Getting back at her brother only sweetened the deal.

I knew that he had heard about us too. I saw it on his face the moment he walked in through the locker room door. He pushed by his friends, the fucking fake-ass pussies that stuck by his side when everything went down.

He stepped up to me, a good four or five inches shorter than I was, and I made sure to look down at him as he spoke.

"What the fuck do you think you're doing, Beck?"

Oh, he was mad? Good. I wanted him to be fucking raging by the time I got done destroying him and his fucked-up family.

"Getting ready for practice." I threw my pants into my locker and grabbed my practice jersey. "What are you doing?"

"Don't act cute. You know what the fuck I'm talking about."

How he thought he had the right to speak to me that way, let alone speak to me at all, was something I would never understand. But here we are. Him spraying spit with every word that came out of his mouth, and me not giving one fuck about what he was saying. He may have gotten a pass when it came to our fathers, but he didn't get one from me. I didn't give a shit what he said. His words were pointless. He was dead to me in every sense. And he would have been if I hadn't been pulled off of him when I fucked him up. But smashing his face like I did, didn't even touch the surface. It wouldn't even take the edge off the rage I felt toward him and his disgusting father.

"You mean your sister? Hmm, what's her name? Jodie? Jane? Oh, wait. Sweet, sweet Josie. She tastes just as sweet as her name," I replied casually, but I saw his anger building. His nostrils flared and his hands shook at his sides.

"Leave her alone, Beck. I don't want her around trash like you."

"Trash like me?" I laughed, but there was no humor, and I didn't miss the way Olly stood up or how Carson made his way toward us from the locker room door.

"Your sister seems to like my trash." I leaned forward for only him to hear. "She was screaming my name over and over again yesterday." I stared down at him and dared him to say a fucking word. "She was begging me for it."

He held my eyes, staring up at me with disgust pulsating his features. I grabbed his t-shirt and slammed my chest against his.

"Begging. For. It," I hissed. "And there's not a damn thing you can do about it. Unless you want your precious sister to know all about the fucked-up filth her name holds. What's it going to be?"

"Fuck you." He shoved away from my chest, and I let him go.

My blood was boiling inside my veins and my temper was good for no one. In the end, I would fuck over the Voses, and I would hit them exactly where it hurt.

Because there was nothing Joseph Vos loved more than his own name and legacy. He admired power and money, and his name was the greatest power he had. And his name was something Lucas almost ruined.

He would have ruined it too if I hadn't let my own rage get the best of me. When I found out what Lucas had done, I couldn't be stopped.

No one could pull me from him as I slammed my fist into his flesh like a madman.

I couldn't even remember anyone else being there until four police officers pulled me off Lucas after they had witnessed what I had done.

And Joseph Vos took advantage of that fact. His son had committed the crime, but I was the one who got arrested.

A son for a son. It was the deal they had made.

Apparently, it was the deal they used to protect us both.

A deal I refused to live by.

I was going to handle it on my own.

My father would be furious, but that was a risk I had to take.

He wanted some quick revenge with Josie and then I would forget it all and move on and things would be peachy again between our families. But I wasn't here to play tit for tat.

He had warned me again to stay away from her after our golf expedition yesterday. His exact words were, "She's a nice girl."

No part of me hesitated because she was a nice girl.

If anything, I didn't want to hurt her because she was the exact opposite of what they expected her to be. She was the exact opposite of any of them.

But she was still a Vos, her father's blood ran through her veins, and that was something I couldn't forget. Unfortunately, Josie Vos would be the most beautiful collateral damage Clermont Bay had ever seen.

I jerked my jersey over my head and pulled on my shorts. Olly was still watching Lucas where he stood on the opposite side of the locker room as I sat down and started pulling on my cleats.

Today was our first practice of the year. We wouldn't have a game for several more weeks, but we all took this seriously. Even though I just fucking wanted to leave. I couldn't imagine how I was going to deal with seeing Lucas's face every day. It was bad enough that I still had to go to school with him. Being on a team with him was something else entirely.

He was our pitcher, and a poor one at that.

I grabbed my bag and slammed my locker shut. Carson and Olly were on my tail as we headed out to the field. I didn't know if they felt like they always had to be on high alert when I was around Lucas, but it probably wasn't a bad idea.

Because no one else would be able to stop me if something happened between us again. I wasn't even sure if they could. We stepped onto the grass and Carson looked behind us.

"I can't believe that motherfucker had enough nerve to even speak to you." Carson threw his hat on backward before grabbing his glove.

"He's lucky we're at school." I shook out my hands to try to calm the rage that was still flowing inside of me before putting my glove on.

"He's lucky we haven't killed him." Olly tossed his bag on the ground with more force than necessary. "I can't wait until we graduate, and I never have to look at him again."

"But I will." I chuckled without humor and grabbed a ball. "You all know Vos is going to be up his daddy's ass for as long as he can manage."

"Fuck him." Carson caught the ball and threw it back. "And fuck his daddy issues."

"Speaking of daddy issues." Olly finally grabbed his glove as Coach came on the field. "What happened with Josie?"

"Nothing." I shrugged, but they both knew I was full of shit. That was the one thing about us. We had never been able to lie to one another. No matter how hard we tried.

"You're so full of shit. She walked up to that locker this morning all goo-goo eyed, and you looked like you crushed her when you kissed Cami."

I didn't want to think about why my chest felt tight at his words. "I didn't kiss Cami. Cami kissed me."

"Either way." Olly stretched his arms over his head and nodded to Coach as he passed. "The girl looked heartbroken. You already fuck her?"

"No." I held the ball against my hip and looked at him. "You all would know if I fucked her."

"You had to do something." He shrugged. "That girl looked dickmatized."

"Whatever." I chuckled and threw the ball back to Carson.

"So, you're not denying it." Carson picked up right where Olly left off. The two of them weren't going to drop this until I gave them something. I knew it, but I still didn't want to tell them. For some reason, I wanted to keep everything about her to myself. "She's definitely dickmatized."

"My dick has not been in her." I held my arms out. "Are you happy?"

"He said dick." Olly was talking straight to Carson now. "So, he's had other things in her."

I rolled my eyes and was thankful when Coach called us all to the dirt.

They would know when I had been inside Josie Vos, truly inside her. But for now, I was giving her what she needed. I was taking from her what I desired.

I would be selfish with her until I earned her trust, then I would crush everything that ever existed between us. She would hate me, and I would live with that fact.

I could live with her hate far better than I could live with Frankie's sadness.

But I knew how fucked up that was. I knew what I was doing wasn't right. Lucas had done far worse than use Frankie, but the similarities in what I was doing to Josie made my chest feel like it was on fire.

Nothing about what I was doing was rational. I hadn't been

able to think clearly since I had found out what he did, and I didn't have space for rational thinking right now.

If I did, if I let myself think about the choices I was making and repercussions I would have to face, I would cave.

If I thought too much about Josie, I would abandon my entire plan.

But I was already too far gone to change my mind.

I would deal with the consequences of every fucked-up decision I made.

CHAPTER
FIFTEEN

I had been avoiding Beck since yesterday.

He had text me at the end of the day to see how the rest of my day went, but I didn't respond. When he text me two more times later in the evening, I had turned my phone off.

I couldn't focus with him. With his presence or his texts or the memories I kept playing over and over in my head.

"So you're still mad at me?" Lucas jogged up beside me as the two of us headed into school. I overslept after tossing and turning most of the night, and I wasn't in the mood to be late or to deal with Lucas.

"Well, you were a complete asshole." I looked over at him. "Why are we having this conversation right now?"

"Because you've been ignoring me at home."

He had a point. I had been. I had been ignoring everyone and everything.

I had no idea what to think or feel. I felt like I was constantly at war in my own head. My father and Lucas and even Lucas's mother were now my family, whether I liked it or not. They were all I had, regardless of how much I hated it.

And Beck hated my family.

He hated them, and a part of me believed that he truly hated me as well. It didn't matter that I felt more alive when I was with him than I had since my mother passed. He had been cruel and vindictive, and he had a girlfriend, and I had let myself feel more secure when I was with him than with anyone else.

But Beck saw me.

He saw me when everyone else was seeing what they wanted, and I had convinced myself that meant something it didn't.

"I'm sorry. Okay?" Lucas straightened his jacket, and he looked so perfect in his uniform. He was bred for this lifestyle.

"It's fine." I shook my head, but I couldn't shake the feeling of unease as I looked at him. I knew that he didn't like Beck, but when I heard him talking about me to my father, I had lost trust in him.

A trust that was fragile to begin with.

We walked through the front doors, and I felt like more people were looking at me now than they had yesterday. But yesterday curiosity filled their eyes and the questions on their lips, today it felt like nothing but judgment.

I had only been here one day, and already, they thought they knew who I was.

I pushed through them quickly with Lucas at my side, and he stopped by my locker as I quickly traded out books.

"I've just had a lot on my mind." His hands fidgeted with his pockets. "Dad puts a lot of pressure on me."

I hated that he said that. It felt like a dig that started at the base of my spine and slowly worked its way up. I knew that he hadn't meant anything by it, but he was right. My father did have expectations of him, and suddenly, he thought he could have expectations for me too.

But it was different.

Whatever Lucas and my dad shared, it was something I would never have with him.

It was something that I would never allow.

Because when I looked at him, all I could see was how much my mother had loved him. Even to the end, even through all his faults, I think a part of her still loved the idea of him until the day she died.

"I know." I nodded and closed my locker. I didn't want to fight with Lucas. I didn't need anything else to complicate my life or my head.

"Fuck," Lucas swore under his breath, and I turned just in time to see Beck walking toward us.

He had to see Lucas standing right next to me, but he wasn't looking at him. He was staring daggers at me as he pushed through the sea of students.

"I'm going to get to class." I lifted my backpack over my shoulder with shaking hands, but I was too late. Beck was already in front of us, and there wasn't a chance I was going to be able to escape without his notice.

I ignored him as he moved in front of me, but Lucas didn't. His body was stiff and he was looking at Beck with as much animosity as Beck was looking at me.

"Why didn't you answer me last night?" Beck wasn't quiet, and I saw several people turn their heads to see what he was saying.

"You called me?" I cocked my head slightly and tucked a piece of hair behind my ear.

"Don't act dumb." His pupils swelled as he looked down at me.

I pulled my phone out of my pocket and flipped it over in my hand. "Oh." I looked up at him with fake shock on my face. "I must have turned it off."

He bit out a harsh laugh, but I didn't care if he was angry.

"Come on, Josie. I'll walk you to class."

Beck's gaze snapped to Lucas when he spoke, but I was already moving. I pushed past Beck, my shoulder grazing against his chest, and I followed Lucas toward my class.

Beck's hand wrapped around my bicep before I could get too far, and he looked torn as his gaze bounced from me to Lucas and back.

"Turn on your phone," he commanded me, and I jerked my arm from his touch.

"You don't get to tell me what to do."

I didn't give him another moment to respond. I pushed past him and walked to my class without a backward glance.

He had some nerve.

I was so angry with him. So fed up. My heart raced as I said goodbye to Lucas and took my seat next to Cami. I could barely even look at her as my hands shook.

She could deal with Beck and his whiplash from now on. I wanted nothing to do with him.

Even if that felt like a lie.

I was determined to believe it. I was determined to keep myself as far from him as possible.

I knew that he wouldn't allow it though. He hadn't allowed it since the moment I met him.

"Hey. You okay?" I looked over at Cami, and there was so much concern in her eyes that all I could feel was guilt.

Guilt over what I had done with Beck, and guilt over the way he had treated her.

"Yeah." I nodded. "I just have a headache." It wasn't a complete lie. My head was pounding.

"Okay." She nodded once and glanced up at the teacher. "You're coming to my house tomorrow before the party. You need to relax."

Her party. Crap. I had completely forgotten about that. I couldn't even believe that she still wanted me to come after the way she was looking at Beck when he had walked off with me yesterday.

"I don't know," I whispered and rubbed my forehead. "I'm not sure the party is such a good idea."

"Come on." She held up her hands as if she was begging. "I promise we'll have a good time."

I should have told her no, but I would be lying if I said I didn't want to get to know her more. I wanted to know what her relationship was like with Beck, or their lack of a relationship if he was to be believed.

But he wasn't.

I couldn't believe anything he said.

"I'll think about it."

She smiled and went back to paying attention to the teacher, but I couldn't focus on anything.

I pulled my phone out and turned it on for the first time

since yesterday afternoon. Message after message popped up on my screen. I ignored the ones from Beck and quickly clicked on Allie's name.

I miss you. She followed it with a crying emoji, and I felt the same way.

School had only been back for two days, but already I felt like it had been forever since I had seen her.

Same. Will you go to a party with me Friday night?

Her response was instant. **Duh.**

I smiled and finally clicked over to Beck's messages.

Are you ignoring me?

Josie.

I can't stop thinking about you.

That last message was the sole reason I should have never looked. One little text message, and my chest tightened. Beck had plenty of things to think about other than me, and I needed to remember that.

It didn't matter what he said.

All that mattered was what he did.

And I couldn't trust him.

I tucked my phone back in my pocket and tried my hardest to concentrate on what the teacher was saying. But as every minute of the class ticked on, my heart began to race, and my headache worsened. I was going to have to deal with Beck in my next class.

I was going to have to deal with him over and over again, and I was going to have to figure out how to not be affected by him.

But I wasn't sure if I could do that.

When the bell rang, I stuffed my things in my bag and shuffled out of the classroom before Cami could catch me. I moved to the bathroom and stared at myself in the mirror of the packed room.

"You're Josie, right?" Some girl I had never seen before asked as she applied lipstick to her lips.

"That's me."

She smirked before slowly placing the lid on her lipstick and turning toward me. "I heard about you and Beck. Ouch."

I narrowed my eyes and tried to calm the urge to run.

"What are you talking about?"

"Him and Cami. You and him." Her gaze flicked over me, and I knew that she was watching for any sort of reaction. "The rest of us already knew the score when we'd been with Beck, but I heard that you looked shocked."

Nausea rolled in my stomach, and I swallowed the heavy saliva in my mouth. "I haven't been with Beck."

"Oh." She acted genuinely shocked. "Then it's a good thing you found out now."

There were other girls moving around the bathroom, in and out of the stalls, vying for a fraction of the mirrors, and I could tell they were all listening to our conversation.

"Thank you for the heads-up, but there's nothing going on between us." And there never would be.

"Good." She nodded. "I think Cami knows about most of us." She winced as if she was actually ashamed, and my nausea threatened to boil over. Beck had been with this girl? She had known him intimately, and I was... I had no idea what I was. "They are on again, off again all the time, but he always goes back to her."

He always goes back to her.

I had no idea if her sole intention was to wound me, but she had. No matter what I thought I did or didn't feel for Beck, her words had sliced through me and my breath caught in my throat.

The warning bell rang, indicating that we were going to be late for class, and she quickly grabbed her things. I didn't look at her again as I moved. I barely saw anyone.

All I could see was him with her, with Cami, with me.

Beck could have any girl he wanted, and apparently, he did.

I shouldn't have been shocked by that fact. He was who he was, and there was nothing that would happen to change that.

I moved into the classroom and as soon as I looked up, I saw him. He was staring at me, watching the doorway for when I arrived, and I felt like I couldn't breathe as I stared at him.

I avoided his side of the room altogether and quickly claimed a seat as far away from him as I could.

I could still feel him staring at me, but I didn't dare look up.

Beck was bad for me. He was bad, and I knew it.

It was right there in front of my face, and I couldn't be an idiot about that fact anymore.

Whatever game he was playing, I was done.

CHAPTER
SIXTEEN

"My friend Allie is going to meet us here if that's okay." I sat on Cami's bed and looked around her room.

"That's fine." She came out of the closet holding a dress that looked tiny. "There will be a ton of people here tonight."

"Everyone from school?" I hadn't really gotten to know anyone yet. Not other than the nosy questions and the uninvited stories about Beck. And there had been plenty. The girl in the bathroom had only been the first.

Apparently, people thought it was their place to keep me informed.

It didn't matter that Cami liked me, or at least she was acting like she did. Every trip to the bathroom, a girl stopped me to tell me about how heartbroken Cami was when she heard that Beck had something going on with me. I assured them all that there was nothing going on.

Because there wasn't.

Not anymore.

"Yeah. The whole school will be here, a few people from Clermont High, and a few guys that have already graduated." She held the dress up to her body and looked at herself in the mirror as she turned this way and that. "I'm going to set you up with someone."

She looked giddy, as if the thought had just come to her, but I knew better. I knew this was her way of telling me that Beck was off-limits to me, and she was going to try her best to make me off-limits to him.

"I don't know about that." I laughed and pulled a pair of jeans out of my bag. I hadn't realized the attire for her party was going to be so dressy. I hadn't brought anything that even compared to her dress.

"It will be good for you. There's some real eye candy coming tonight." She winked at me in the mirror before turning in my direction and eyeing my jeans. "It doesn't have to be anything serious."

"I'll think about it." That was the most I would give her even though it was a lie. If Beck had taught me anything, it was that a guy during my senior year in Clermont Bay wasn't a good idea. It didn't matter how good of eye candy he was.

But Cami didn't need to know all that. She didn't need to know that her boyfriend/non-boyfriend would be my first and last hook up in this town. I felt bad enough about it on my own.

"What else did you bring?" She nodded toward my jeans, and I winced as I brought out a black band t-shirt. "I can work with this."

I didn't have a clue what she meant until she pulled out a pair of scissors and ran them along the knee of my jeans. I reached out to stop her before I remembered that to girls like her, clothing was nothing. It didn't matter that I had worked for about four hours to be able to pay for those jeans.

It was nothing but fabric to her. Just like I was just another girl to her boyfriend.

By the time Cami got finished restyling my jeans and me, I looked almost unrecognizable in the mirror.

If Cami didn't like me, she wasn't showing it. She had made me look the best I had ever looked. She had ripped my jeans in a way that made them look like they were meant to be that way, my band t-shirt was knotted at my waist, and the smallest sliver of my stomach was showing. She had lined my eyes with a slick black eyeliner that winged out at the sides, and she had left my lips perfectly nude.

I felt good. Even if none of these people liked me except for Allie. I still wanted to impress them.

And even though I shouldn't, I wanted Beck to see me too. I wanted him to see me and regret the things he had done. I wanted him to regret lying to me about Cami and everything else that had ever passed his lips.

Cami, who looked like she was bred for this life. She was in a skin-tight dress that I would never be able to pull off. It was barely longer than my t-shirt had been before she tied it up.

But she looked incredible. Her blonde hair was piled on her head in a large bun and her makeup was flawless.

I understood why Beck would want her. I was sure the entire school did too. Cami was gorgeous, and she knew it. She was confident and didn't seem to care what anyone thought of her.

She was so vastly different from me.

Her friends were the same. I knew that their names were Becca and Ashley, but I couldn't remember which one was which. They hadn't really spoken to me much since we had been here. They were clearly comfortable in Cami's house, but they didn't seem comfortable with me.

I tried to not let that bother me.

These girls were temporary in my life. They didn't matter.

By the time we left her room for the party, there were already a dozen or more people hanging around. I had a feeling that Cami's must have been a normal party spot because no one seemed to feel out of place. They were pouring drinks from her makeshift bar on the dining room table and laughing as the music beat through speakers.

I had no idea how Cami wasn't worried about her house. The place was massive and covered in decor that I knew had to cost a fortune, but she didn't seem concerned at all as she poured us both vodka and soda into cups.

I accepted the drink without a complaint and took a quick sip as I checked my phone. Allie was on her way, but I needed her here now.

I may have had to suffer school without her, but I refused to suffer this party.

"Josie, this is Chad." I was leaning against the wall as Cami walked up to me with a guy I had never seen before. If he went to Clermont Bay Prep, I didn't recognize him.

"Chad. This is Josie." I pushed off the wall and reached out my hand to him when he pushed his in my direction.

"It's nice to meet you, Chad."

"Likewise." He was handsome and his smile was kind.

"Do you go to Prep?" I took another sip of the drink and tried to calm my nerves.

"I did." He nodded. "I graduated last year."

"Oh, cool." I scanned the growing crowd. It felt a little weird that he would still want to be partying with a bunch of high schoolers, but I guess these were his friends.

"You going to Prep? I swear I would have remembered you." He grinned and his eyes sparked with mischief.

I nodded at his question and smiled. "It's my first year there."

"The new girl?" He chuckled. "That can be a bit rough."

"Yeah. They aren't gentle."

He laughed at that, truly laughed, and his smile revealed the smallest dimple on his cheek. Chad was more than just handsome. Something about him seemed charming, even.

But I couldn't stop myself from comparing him to Beck.

His eyes seemed dull compared to Beck's hazel ones that held so much emotion. His smile almost fake.

I knew that was harsh. I knew that the way he smiled at me had nothing to do with Beck, but my stomach didn't tighten when he grinned. My heart rate didn't kick up.

"Hey, girl." Allie walked up, and I couldn't stop smiling as I looked at her outfit. She was the only other girl I had seen so far who was also wearing jeans. She still looked amazing, but she somehow made me feel more at ease.

She made me feel like I wasn't a complete outsider.

"Hi." I hugged her, and she whispered in my ear.

"Who's this tool?"

I couldn't stop my small laugh as I turned her toward Chad. "Allie, this is Chad. Chad, Allie."

"It's nice to meet you, Allie." He gave her the exact same smile he had been giving me.

"You too. Wait." She snapped her fingers. "I think I know you. Did you play baseball last year?"

"I did." His grin became even larger.

"I thought so. We almost smoked you guys."

I couldn't stop smiling as his fell.

"You a Clermont High girl?"

"Guilty." She did a little curtsy, and God, I was so glad she was here.

"Captain." Carson walked up behind Chad and slapped him on the back. "I didn't realize you'd be here tonight."

If Carson was here, that meant Beck wouldn't be far behind. I couldn't stop myself from searching behind Carson for him. I didn't care if he knew what I was doing. I just didn't want to be surprised when he walked in. I didn't want to be caught off guard.

"Let's go grab a drink." Allie pulled her gaze away from Carson to talk to me, but Carson was staring at her. He looked pissed off. Like he didn't want to see her here, maybe us, but I didn't really care what he thought.

I linked my arm in Allie's. "It was nice to meet you, Chad. I'll see you around later?"

"For sure." He smiled again, and now all I could think about was how different it was from *his*. He was already ruining this for me, and he wasn't even here yet.

Allie and I walked arm in arm through the party, and I was surprised by how many people had accumulated so quickly. I had no idea where Cami was. She had disappeared the moment she dropped Chad at my feet.

"Where did you find him?" She looked at me like I was insane, but I thought he seemed nice.

"Cami."

"Of course, you did." She rolled her eyes. She hadn't said

anything about Cami when I told her that she had been friendly to me at school, but I could tell that she wasn't her biggest fan.

"He seems nice."

"He seems like a douche." She pulled me to the table and grabbed a bottle of liquor. "Plus, he went to Prep."

"I go to Prep." I chuckled.

"Semantics." She waved me off. "You're nothing like the rest of them."

She had a point there.

"I can find you a nice, hot Clermont High guy if you're interested."

"I'm not interested." I grabbed the drink she handed me and took a sip. I had no idea what it was, but it tasted far better than what Cami had made.

"Because of Beck." She waggled her eyebrows, and I slapped her arm.

"No. Because I'm not interested."

"Okay." She winked at me because she knew better than anyone else how I was feeling. I hadn't told her the full extent of what had happened between the two of us, but she knew enough.

"Plus." I leaned closer to her. "Beck is off-limits, remember?"

"Not according to him."

"He's a liar." That fact was plain and simple.

"Who's a liar?"

We jumped at the sound of Beck's voice, and I whirled in his direction. My heart skyrocketed without even seeing him.

"No one." My answer came out so quickly that even I felt suspicious.

"Okay." He looked between Allie and me. "You've been avoiding me."

I took a long sip of my drink to try to calm myself down. "I haven't been avoiding you. I've been busy."

He was looking me over, checking me out without even trying to hide it, and Allie was smiling like a fool. "Doing what?"

"Work. School. Hanging out with your girlfriend."

Allie snorted out a laugh and almost choked on her drink. But Beck didn't seem affected.

He didn't care that I knew about her.

He apparently thought I wouldn't care, but he was wrong.

"You look gorgeous tonight. Has anyone told you that?" His eyes looked so possessive. He looked at me like he wanted me, like he didn't care that I had just mentioned his fucking girlfriend.

Even though both of us knew the truth. But that truth didn't stop the butterflies from taking off in my stomach.

"Don't." I started to speak just as Allie did.

"Chad Johnson did. He was practically drooling over her when I got here."

I wanted to punch Allie.

"Chad Johnson?" Beck made a face and part of me thought he might be a little jealous. "He's almost twenty and still hanging out at high school parties."

"So, what?" I pushed some hair behind my ear. "His opinion must be wrong?"

"No." He shook his head, and I noticed his eyes seemed darker than before. Chad's eyes weren't only duller than Beck's, they were nothing compared to his. "I said you looked gorgeous."

He needed to quit saying that. I couldn't think straight when he said things that he shouldn't be saying.

"There you are." Cami wrapped her arm around Beck's shoulder and smiled. He tensed under her touch. It was minute, but it was there. I didn't know if it was simply because I was watching or if it was something more.

He had to know that I would see them together tonight.

He had to know that I wasn't going to just sit here and let him tell me I was gorgeous, then have to watch him with her.

"Josie, what'd you think of Chad?" She didn't seem to notice or care that Beck was tense. She ran her fingers through the base of his hair like it was the most natural thing for her to be doing. Like her hands were so used to touching him.

"He seems nice." It wasn't a lie. He did. He just wasn't my type. I was apparently into men who were a bit more toxic.

A lot more toxic, actually.

"He really liked you." She winked at me. "He asked me for your number."

Beck was staring straight ahead at me, and I felt like his eyes were burning. If he was angry, he had no right to be. He had no right to anything when it came to me.

"I gave it to him, of course." She smiled.

"Of course." Allie said it so quietly only I could hear.

"Thanks." I smiled and tried to avoid looking back at Beck. She was still touching him, and he was letting her. It didn't matter what he had said about there being nothing between him and Cami. The proof was right here in front of me.

Even if they were on and off.

I refused to be anything at all. Not like this.

"I heard he was a bit of a baseball star. He better than you, Beck?" I cocked my head to the side.

"Are you fucking with me right now? He's still in Clermont Bay. Isn't he?"

"You're staying here too." Cami chuckled, and Beck went stock-still. "That doesn't mean anything."

Beck was staying here? I figured he'd be long gone after he graduated. I was sure he had his choice of Ivy League schools just waiting for him.

"I'm going to get a drink." Beck shrugged Cami off of him and walked past us all without another word.

I didn't know why I suddenly felt bad for him, but he seemed so lost with these people. He seemed so different.

I knew that I was the one who probably didn't know anything real about him. These people had been his friends forever. Cami had been more.

But part of me still felt like I somehow knew him better, that I was the one who had been privy to the real him, and I knew how stupid that made me.

Beck only let people see what he wanted them to see. He made me see him as something that he wasn't. All for what?

To get in my pants? To make my brother angry because he fucked me? Was that his end game here?

I wanted to follow after him and demand he give me answers, but this wasn't the place or time. Cami's face looked tight and uncomfortable, and I wondered what it had to be like to be her. She was the queen of Clermont Prep. Everyone loved her. If they didn't, they worshipped her. She had everything at her fingertips.

Everything she could ever want. Including Beck.

But she still didn't seem happy.

"I'm going to go smoke." She pulled a joint out of the top of her dress. "Anyone want to join?"

"No. Thank you." I held up my drink. "This will probably kick my ass on its own."

She gave me a smile that didn't meet her eyes before she walked out the door.

"I don't like that girl." Allie was already pouring herself another drink, and I couldn't blame her. So far, this was the most awkward party I had ever been to.

"I can tell." I set my cup down on the table. "Maybe we should just leave."

"I just got here." She looked up at me, and I could see the

sympathy on her face. I hated that look more than anything. "But we can go."

"No." I shook my head and smiled. "Make another drink. I'm fine."

"You sure?"

"Yes." I nodded and waggled my eyebrows at her. "Plus, how am I going to meet anymore Chads if we go home."

I had no interest in meeting anymore Chads, or any other boys for that matter, but she didn't need to know that. I just wanted her to have a good time, and if that meant I had to suffer through a few more hours at this party, I would.

I had asked her to be here with me, and she hadn't even hesitated.

The two of us stuck to each other's sides as we mingled and laughed.

And after about an hour, I almost forgot about Beck altogether.

Not really, but I hadn't seen him.

It wasn't until the two of us went outside to get a breath of fresh air that I ran into him again.

Beck had clearly been drinking. There were people all around us, and I could barely see his eyes against the pitch-black night. The lights that hung over Cami's back yard did little to light it up.

"Allie, what's the deal with you and Carson anyway?" It was the first words he had spoken to us since earlier with Cami, and he still wasn't talking to me.

"There is no deal." Allie stopped in front of him and seemed so uncomfortable by his question.

"Oh. There definitely is." He leaned back in his chair and his beer bottle was held precariously between his fingers. His hair was in disarray, and I wondered if it had been his fingers to make it that way or Cami's. Or some other girl at this party. "Don't you think so, Josie?"

My stomach dropped when he said my name. "She said there's not."

"But girls lie." He leaned forward and put his elbows on his knees. "Don't they?"

Everyone around us was watching, and I wished he would just go back to ignoring me. Things were much easier then.

"Maybe the ones you're used to." I had no idea why I said it. I heard a few chuckles and gasps around me, but I didn't care.

He looked away from me and brought his attention back to Allie. "I think he likes you."

"I think you're drunk."

"Oh." He pointed his beer bottle in her direction. "You are correct about that."

"Your brother's here," Allie ignored Beck and whispered in my ear.

I looked over my shoulder, and sure enough, Lucas was in the house talking and laughing.

I hadn't seen him since we first arrived. He had told me he wasn't sure if he would be here.

Carson walked up as if he already knew, and he quickly looked between us and Beck.

"Beck, man. It's time to go."

"Oh, no." He shook him off. "Josie was finally talking to me for the first time tonight. I can't leave now."

"I talked to you earlier," I clarified, but he wasn't having any of it.

"About Chad." He snapped his fingers as if he suddenly remembered. "How could I forget that you were suddenly so into Chad Johnson?"

"Am I not allowed to be into Chad Johnson?" I had no idea why I was challenging him when he was like this, but he was pissing me off. He had no right to be jealous of any other guy.

Especially some guy I didn't give two shits about.

"He's a prick, so no." He took a long drink from his beer, and Carson looked stressed.

"Who should I be into then, Beck?" I looked around the party. "Would Carson be better? Or maybe Olly?"

His dark eyes stared me down as I said his friends' names, but I wasn't scared of him. He didn't just get to be an ass simply because he wanted to.

I turned my attention away from him and looked at his friend. "Carson?"

"You wouldn't fucking dare."

My gaze snapped back to him. "Wouldn't I?" I pointed to my chest. "I'm single, and as far as I know, so is he."

"Josie," Allie whispered my name in warning, but I didn't heed it. I just kept pushing and pushing until he did something other than sit there and act like he was some sort of fucking saint. Like he hadn't used me to get exactly what he wanted.

"That's the difference here, Clermont. I can figure out if I'm single or not. Can you?"

"You didn't seem to care how single I was when you were riding my fingers."

There were shocked inhales, a ring of chuckles, and a whispered 'Oh, fuck.'

I wasn't sticking around to listen though. I pushed away from Allie and headed toward the door. I couldn't believe he would fucking say that.

In front of all these people.

I couldn't believe he would fucking dare.

I was so angry, I could feel tears burning the back of my eyes, but I refused to cry.

There was noise behind me, what sounded like people moving, but I didn't look back. I pushed through the crowd and headed back into Cami's house. I found her room as quickly as I could and grabbed my bag. She had asked me to stay the night here, but there was no way in hell.

I needed to leave, and I needed to leave now. I text Allie and let her know I was leaving, and she said she was right behind me.

I hated leaving her, but I couldn't stay here a moment longer.

I couldn't be here with him.

I caught Lucas's eyes as I made my way back down the stairs, and he moved over to me quickly. I didn't have the energy to deal with him tonight either.

"You okay?" He was following me as I walked outside the door.

"I'm fine." I shoved my key into the keyhole on my door and ripped the driver's side door open. "I'm heading back to the house."

"Have you been drinking?" Lucas actually seemed concerned, and I hesitated at the door. I had been drinking but I hadn't had any in a while. I felt completely sober after talking to Beck.

"I'm good to drive. I promise."

"Of course, you're out here." Beck's laughter was slurred and shadowed by Carson's cursing. "It's my favorite Vos and my least favorite Vos."

"Come on, man." Olly tugged on Beck's arm, but neither one of them could control him. He was heading straight for my car on unsteady legs.

He pushed his hands on the hood of the car, directly across from where I stood next to Lucas. "I'm sorry for saying that."

"What did he say?" Lucas puffed his chest, and he stared at Beck like he wanted to kill him.

I pushed him back and stared at Beck. "You're not sorry."

"I am." He looked at me. He looked like he was sincere, but I wasn't going to believe him.

"Who's taking him home?" I looked at Carson and Olly.

"Frankie's coming to pick him up soon."

I nodded and turned back to Lucas, but he was still staring at Beck. "Stay the fuck away from her."

It was the wrong thing to say. Beck was far too intoxicated to deal with his anger toward Lucas.

"Her?" Beck nodded his head toward me. "Fucking make me."

Lucas moved like he was going to confront him, but I stepped in his way. There was no way I was going to let him put his hands on Beck, or Beck put his hands on him.

This was going too far, and I wouldn't stand here and watch them fight.

Beck moved around the hood of my car, and I knew that if he got his hands on Lucas, none of us would be able to stop him.

Olly and Carson grabbed his shoulders, but they wouldn't have stood a chance.

"Put him in my car." I pointed at Olly as I dared Lucas to say a word.

Olly and Carson jerked Beck backward and pushed him toward my passenger side.

"I'm not a fucking child." Beck was pushing against Olly before he slammed my passenger side door.

"I'll see you at the house." I pointed at a still fuming Lucas.

I was so damn angry by the time I got my own door closed that I couldn't talk. Beck Clermont was sitting there riding in the car I had borrowed from my dad with his perfect face and perfect life. If he wasn't so drunk, I would yell at him. I would demand that he tell me what the hell his problem was and demand that he leave me the hell alone.

But he was angry too.

I could feel his rage still radiating off his body. He wanted to say something. He wanted to scream and shout and fight, and for whatever reason, he didn't.

"Did you and Lucas have a fight over a girl?"

He laughed, but there wasn't a single ounce of humor in it.

"Cami?" I asked. I didn't know why but the thought of him being so worked up over Cami pissed me off.

"No." He shook his head, and I wanted to ask him more about her. Why was he with me right now, when he could have been there with her? "It wasn't Cami. Turn here."

He pointed to the right, and I quickly made the turn. We were going in the opposite direction of our houses.

"I'm taking you home, Beck."

"I just need to make a quick stop."

I huffed but I had already made the turn. I was anxious as it was, considering I had been drinking earlier in the night, and I tightened my hands on the steering wheel as I drove down the dark road.

It was lined with trees on one side and the ocean on the other. The view was so beautiful. The moon was high in the sky, and it reflected off the water in a million diamonds of light. The water looked so peaceful and calm, a complete contrast to the world that hid beneath.

I glanced at Beck's face as he stared out the window. It reminded me so much of him. He was so vast and an endless depth of secrets. It didn't matter what I thought I knew about him; there would always be more that I didn't know. There would always be so much more that he was hiding.

We rounded a large curve, and the golf course came into view. I had never driven this way to the club, and I wouldn't have taken it if I knew this was where he was leading us.

"The club?" I asked, and he turned from the ocean to look at it.

"Yeah. Just a quick stop."

I pulled into the parking lot, and it was weird how quiet and empty it seemed. This place was always brimming with employees and members, and it almost seemed eerie without a soul here.

Beck opened his door and climbed out. I followed quickly behind him, mostly because I didn't want to be left in the car on my own.

"We can't be here right now," I whisper-shouted at him. I had no idea why I was whispering, but I felt like we were going to get in trouble.

He reached his hand into his pocket, and for the first time in what felt like forever, a genuine smile lit up his face as he pulled out the keys. "I have the keys, princess."

He shoved them into the door, and I looked behind us. It didn't matter that his dad owned this place. I still felt like we were doing something wrong. Like we were doing something that could easily get me fired.

We pushed through the door, and Beck quickly punched numbers into the security system that chirped at us. His fingers were clumsy, but it quit the moment he hit Enter.

He gripped my fingers in his and moved through the dark hallway with ease.

"Where are we going?" I followed after him as we passed the dining room and moved into the main hallway. He didn't answer me. He just kept walking with my hand in his and determination on his face.

We pushed through a door that led to the pool, and I dug in my heels.

"Beck."

"What?" He dropped my hand and tugged at the base of his t-shirt. I watched him as he lifted it over his head, struggling as he got to his shoulders, and I couldn't stop staring at his toned stomach or the way his muscles disappeared into his jeans.

"We are not doing this."

"Doing what?" He threw his shirt to the side and gripped my fingers in his again. He tugged me toward him as he walked a few steps backward.

"I told your friends that I would take your drunk ass home. Not that I'd let you go drown in a pool."

"You won't let me drown." His fingers were toying with mine, and I could barely concentrate on what he was saying. I couldn't concentrate on anything other than the feel of those damn fingers.

"I am not getting in that pool, Beck."

He dropped my hand as we got to the edge and kicked off one of his shoes. He laughed as he almost tripped, and I cursed as I reached out for him.

"See, Josie." He didn't stop me from holding on to his arms. "You're my little savior."

"I am not your savior." I shook my head. He was even drunker than I thought. "I just don't want your death on my hands."

His other shoe went flying and his hands dropped to his belt. I watched every second of him slipping the leather out of its buckle. His abs bunched and moved with every move of his arms, and even though I told myself I should look away, I couldn't.

He popped the button of his jeans and slowly lowered his zipper. Black boxers still covered him, but I still felt suddenly hot. I felt like I was suddenly crossing a line with him even though I wasn't doing anything wrong.

He tugged his jeans off his hips, and I dropped my hands from his arms.

"Are you coming?" He looked from me to the water. It looked perfectly inviting, the water was crystal clear and lit up from lights beneath it. I could hear the ocean crashing against the sand in the background, but I couldn't see it. All I could see was him.

"Beck, this isn't a good idea." He wasn't listening to me. He dived headfirst into the water. "Shit." I kicked off my shoes in case I had to save his stupid ass, but he glided through the water before quickly coming to the top.

He pushed his dark, wet hair out of his face and grinned at me.

"You worried about me?" He cocked his head to the side and looked at my bare feet.

"Just because I don't like you doesn't mean I want you to drown."

"You like me." He was so sure of himself. He swam toward the edge of the pool and rested his arms on the concrete. "Come in."

"I'm not getting in that water, Beck. Get out."

"I'm not getting out until you get in."

I shook my head and crossed my arms.

"Just put your feet in."

I looked at him and I knew that he wouldn't give up until I did. If Beck was nothing else, he was stubborn.

I tried to roll up the edge of my jeans, but they were too tight against my legs.

"Just take them off." Beck smiled.

"You would like that, wouldn't you?" I tugged them back down toward my ankles.

"I won't even look." He covered his eyes with his hands. "And I promise not to touch you."

He was so full of shit. I knew that with absolute confidence, but it didn't stop me from turning away from him and tugging my t-shirt out of the knot. I undid my jeans and pulled my t-shirt down over my ass before I tugged them down my legs.

I folded them as I took a deep breath and laid them on one of the lounge chairs. Beck was watching my every move as I made my way toward him. His chin was resting on his arms, but his eyes were solely on me.

I sat down next to him and dipped my toes into the cool water. I slowly dragged my feet back and forth and watched the way the water cascaded over my legs. I did everything I could to avoid looking over at him.

"Are you happy now?" I held on to the edge of the pool and glanced over at him.

He was still just staring at me. I didn't know if it was the alcohol or what was going through his head, but the mask he normally wore felt like it was slipping. His eyes looked more green than brown, and he looked like he was perfectly content in that moment. Just sitting there staring at me.

"I am happy."

That should have made me feel good. It should have made me do anything other than becoming overwhelmed with anger. But when I closed my eyes, all I could see was her. Here he was with me breaking rules, basically breaking into the club, and he should have been with her.

"Cami," I said her name, and he let his head fall back between his shoulders in exasperation.

"I don't want to talk about Cami."

"Well, that's too bad, Beck." My hands tightened on the pool's edge. "I feel like Cami is the only thing we should be talking about right now."

He shook his head, but I wasn't finished.

"She's your girlfriend."

"I told you..." He practically growled out the words.

"You belong to her."

"Fine." He pushed his hair out of his face and moved closer to me. He placed his hands on either side of my legs, our fingers only centimeters apart.

He had a silver chain around his neck that I hadn't noticed before. The water glistened off it, and I felt mesmerized as it dangled in the space between us.

"Let's pretend like I am hers. That doesn't stop you from wanting me."

My gaze snapped up to his, and the urge to slap him was unreal. How dare he say something like that to me?

I pushed off the concrete in order to escape him. My leg was only halfway out of the water when his fingers gripped my thighs. "Please don't."

"Don't slap Cami in my face." My thighs shook beneath his touch. "I'm already aware that what we did was wrong."

"Cami doesn't give a shit about me." He tried to push his way between my knees to get closer to me, but I boxed him out.

Beck was already close enough. I couldn't think straight as it was, and every inch closer he got to me fucked with my head a little bit more. I needed to put distance between us. I needed to get away from him.

"She says differently."

"Did she also say my dad was sick?" His fingers dug into my skin. "No?" He chuckled, but I had no idea what he was talking about.

I shook my head softly. "I don't know..."

"Exactly. She didn't tell you because she doesn't know. Cami doesn't care about anything other than her reputation."

"I don't understand." He was talking in circles. I knew that they were supposedly unsteady, but this felt like more.

"Cami uses me, Josie, and I use her."

I tensed as the words passed his lips. I didn't want to think about either one of them using each other. The thought made my chest feel tight and made the urge to run away pump through every part of me.

"So, what? It's just sex?"

He searched my face, and I tried to hide my reaction. I couldn't protect my heart from Beck Clermont if I let him know every one of my secrets. He needed to know that I was unaffected by him and Cami. I needed to make him believe that I didn't care.

"No." He shook his head. "I mean, yes, there has been sex."

I looked away from him because I felt like I was going to snap. There was something inside of me that was pulled so tightly in so many directions, and I felt like another single word from his lips could make it all shatter apart.

"But that's not what it's about."

I bit down on my lip and looked up at the night sky. The stars were so bright that I couldn't believe I hadn't noticed them before. But I had been too busy looking at him to even worry about looking up.

"Cami's fucked up."

I jerked as I listened to him say that about her, but he tightened his hands on my thighs to keep me still.

"Her parents have expectations of her that she will never fulfil. They have pushed her for her entire life, and she's beyond her breaking point."

"So what?" I finally looked back at him. "You cheating on her is supposed to help?"

"You don't understand." He bit down on his bottom lip, and I knew that he was struggling with what to say to me. I didn't know if it was because it hurt him somehow or because he was simply coming up with the lies as he went. "Cami's sleeping with Mr. Weston."

"The art teacher?" I said it so loud I was sure someone was going to know we were here.

"Yes. The art teacher. She's been sleeping with him since we were sophomores."

"I don't understand." I didn't understand anything he was saying. If Cami was sleeping with someone else, why would he still be dating her? Why would he act like he was completely unaffected by her betrayal?

"Nobody knows, Josie." His eyes were a little wild, and I knew he wasn't supposed to be telling me this. For whatever reason, this was Cami's secret that he was willing to keep. "Cami and I are a couple in pretense only. She's in love with a man who's twice her age and married, and I help her keep her secret because Cami has been there for me. As fucked up as that is, Cami doesn't deserve any other bad things in her life."

"So, she fucks a married man and you're her boy toy on the side? That doesn't sound like love." I was beginning to hate Cami. I had resented her before, knowing she had Beck, that he was hers, but now it felt different. I was judging her for something I couldn't understand.

He pressed his fingers into my chin and lifted my face to look at him. "Cami was there for Frankie when no one else was. Cami's not bad."

I shook my head because that still didn't make sense. What did Frankie have to do with anything?

"Cami's in love with a man who has preyed on her weakness. She's obsessed over him, and he goes home and fucks his wife. I know that doesn't make it right, but I don't know how to help her. This is the only way I know how."

"So, she uses you so no one suspects a thing, and you get what? Are you just the hero here?"

"I'm not a fucking hero, Josie." He cupped some water in his hand and let it fall over my knee. "No one suspects anything of her, and I get to do as I please with no expectations."

Realization finally hit me. "You get to fuck whoever you want with no attachments."

He winced but didn't deny a thing. "I told you I wasn't a hero. Cami and I have been the 'it' couple at Prep since we really were dating. We didn't see why we should end a good thing when we could both still get what we wanted."

"You are so fucked up." I pushed up to stand, but this time he gripped my hips and pulled me down into the water with him. I slapped at his shoulder and brought my knees into his stomach as the cool water hit mine. "Let me go, Beck."

I was so angry, and I wanted him away from me. He had

touched me, had brought my body to orgasm, and he expected me to just sit here and be okay with what he was telling me.

I was one of the girls who was supposed to have no expectations.

I was as dispensable as the rest.

"I can't." He ran his nose up my neck while I was trying everything in my power to get away from him. His hands were clinging to me and forcing me against him, and every part of me wanted to melt against his body.

Even though I hated everything he had just said, I still somehow didn't want him to let me go. I pushed against him, begging him to stop, but my heart raced for more.

I knew how fucked up that was. I knew how insane that made me.

But I couldn't stop it.

He kissed the spot where my soaked t-shirt met my neck and I let out the tiniest whimper. He didn't need any more encouragement. Gripping my thighs in his hands, he lifted me and forced them apart as if he couldn't stand another moment away from me.

And I let him.

I let him press against my center, and I didn't say a word as his tongue ran along the length of my neck.

I would deal with the consequences tomorrow. I had known Beck was a bad idea from the beginning, and he was becoming more and more of a mistake the longer I got to know him.

He had made it clear to me that he wasn't the hero, but I had still wanted him to be. I wanted him to be more than what he showed everyone else, more than what he showed me, but I was a fool.

I was as stupid as I had just judged Cami for. I was falling for a guy who was as available to me as Cami's affair was to her.

Both of us knew that it wouldn't end well, but it didn't stop us from falling. Beck was a risk I had been willing to take. He was a risk I knew would destroy me in the end, but I couldn't see that far ahead.

All I could see was him and the way he was looking at me like I was the only thing he needed.

I tightened my legs around his waist and pulled him even closer to me. I wanted to feel him everywhere. I wanted to know that I wasn't just imagining this in my head. I wanted to see him burn for me like I was burning for him.

Because right now, I felt like nothing could stop the searing want inside of me. I had never felt like this before, not even a fraction of this need, and I wanted him to feel it too. I needed him to.

Because he may have thought I was another girl who was nothing to him, but I couldn't believe that. Not at this moment.

Tomorrow, I would clear my head, and I would face the facts head-on.

But tonight?

Tonight, I just wanted to pretend like I wasn't the girl whose entire life had been ruined the moment my mother had left me. I wanted to pretend that I didn't hate everything except for him. I was just a girl who needed him, and he wasn't the guy who was going to ruin me.

I could forget that he wasn't the hero for a little bit longer.

His mouth met mine, and I didn't hold back. I could taste the alcohol on his tongue when it met mine, but I didn't care.

I let him devour my mouth, and I used my legs to push myself against him over and over again. There was barely anything between us, but it still felt like too much.

I gripped the edge of my t-shirt and struggled to pull it over my head. Beck laughed as he helped me, and I couldn't stop myself from laughing with him.

I managed to rip it over my head, and it landed in the water with a loud plop. My simple white bra was practically see-through from the water, and I forced myself not to cover a single inch as he looked his fill.

I had never been checked out so brazenly by a man, and it made me feel crazy. His eyes roaming over my skin made me feel like I was perfect even though I knew that to be so far from the truth.

He lowered his head and pressed his mouth to the swell of my breast. "You are so beautiful." He didn't wait for any reply. He moved to the next breast and pressed his lips there before swiping his tongue beneath the fabric. I felt that move straight to my core.

My hips jolted against his, and I wanted to beg him for more. I wanted to tell him to do whatever he wanted with me.

My back slammed into the pool wall, and I hadn't even realized we were moving. His hips pushed into mine, harder than before, and I moaned as I ran my fingers into his dark hair.

His hands found my ass, and he lifted me up. I tried to cling to him as he pushed me away from him, but Beck was in full control. He set me on the edge of the pool, and he slid his fingers into the sides of my panties.

I leaned back on my hands and lifted my hips as he pulled them off my ass and down my legs. I was fully exposed to him and the cool night air, the only thing between us was the thin fabric of my bra.

He was staring at me like he had never really seen me before, his gaze flicking over every inch of my skin as if he was trying to memorize it, and his eyes didn't meet mine again until they reached the apex of my thighs.

He stared up at me as he pushed my legs apart, and the urge to cover myself was overwhelming. I had never been on display like this for anyone.

I had never allowed someone such intimate access to my body, and I knew that he didn't deserve it.

I was giving that privilege to a man who wouldn't appreciate it, but I still wanted it to be him. Every part of me was sure about that fact.

I wanted him to take whatever part of me he wanted, and I would deal with my regrets later.

Even if he was just a fucked-up boy who had no clue what he truly wanted.

I knew that I wanted him, and it was that simple for me.

"Touch yourself."

My gaze snapped to him, and my thighs pushed against his hands. I didn't know what I had expected from him, but it wasn't that.

I didn't want to touch myself. I wanted him to touch me. I needed him to touch me.

"What?" My voice was shaky and so unsure. I had touched myself plenty of times in the darkness of my bedroom, but never in front of someone. And never when I was on full display.

He gripped one of my hands in his and moved it to the front of my body. I watched him as he pressed my fingers against my sex. I was already so wet, and he pushed his middle finger over mine as he forced me to drag it through my folds until there wasn't a single inch of me that wasn't covered in my moisture.

My harsh breath rang out between us, and I could barely see straight as he moved my finger in small circles against my clit.

"Show me, Josie." He dropped his hand from mine and pressed it back against my thigh. "Show me how you touch yourself when you think of me."

Oh, God.

"Show me how you touched yourself that night I text you."

Why did that sound so dirty? Why did that make my hand start to move like I was at home chasing my orgasm on my own? My fingers moved like I was chasing it for no one but him.

He stared down at my sex as I moved, and his chest heaved in and out with each breath. His hands pushed down on my thighs, widening me farther for him, and I dropped back on my elbow.

His fingers touched my pussy, causing a whimper to rip through me as he pushed inside my body. His hand moved much slower than mine, and I couldn't stop myself as I moved my hips against him. I was chasing every sensation he would give me.

It all felt like too much but not nearly enough.

I was overwhelmed, but I needed more. He stared at me as he lowered his head and pressed a gentle kiss against me. My fingers trembled under his lips, but his found speed. They pushed in and out of me as his tongue snaked its way around my fingers and licked at my clit.

I jolted forward, shocked by the sensation and how good it felt. I had never had anyone touch me like this before. He sucked my clit into his mouth, and I gasped as my eyes rolled back in my head.

I arched my back, trying to force myself closer to him. Closer to the things his wicked mouth was doing.

He pushed my thighs toward me, opening them up to a point that seemed impossible, and I looked back down at him. He was staring at me as he ate me, and I had never seen anything so arousing in all my life.

I tried to breathe as we stared at each other, but it felt impossible. I felt like I couldn't catch my breath or my racing heart or a single thought as they rushed through my mind.

Everything felt centered around where he was touching me. Every part of me focused on him.

His teeth grazed the sensitive skin around my clit before he sucked it back into his mouth, and I felt like he was going to wreck me. He was ravaging me in a way I didn't even know existed. I had touched myself and been touched by others, but none of that felt like this. None of that made me feel like I wouldn't recover when he was through with me.

"Beck, please." I didn't know what I was asking for, but he did. He seemed to know my body far better than I ever could.

He gripped my ass in his hands, and he lifted me up against his mouth. The only part of me touching the ground was my shoulders, but I felt like I needed to get higher.

He sucked my clit into his mouth hard, his fingers digging into my ass at the same time, and I fell apart around him. My thighs slammed shut around his head, and I tried to ride his face even though it all felt like too much.

I couldn't think as my hips bucked and my eyes clenched shut. Every part of me felt like a live wire.

He pulled me down from the pool's edge, and my body slid along his. Every part of him was hard against me, and I squirmed when I felt his hard erection against my stomach.

I had no idea what I was doing, but I knew that I wanted to make him feel like I had just felt. God, like I was still feeling.

I wrapped my arms around his shoulders and my legs around his waist. His hard length pressed against the most sensitive part of me, and I tensed and bit down on my bottom lip.

I wasn't sure I could handle another second of him touching me, but I felt greedy. My body was still reeling from moments before, but I still wanted more.

"You have no idea how gorgeous you are." He ran his finger over my chin and pulled my lip from my teeth before taking it into his own mouth.

His words forced me to tighten my thighs around him. I had never been talked to like that. Not by anyone who didn't have a biased opinion, and there was something about hearing it from his lips that made my chest feel tight with panic.

Those words felt too good coming from his lips. They felt

like he was offering me something more. But I knew better than that.

I let him kiss me, and I forced my panic down with every swipe of his tongue.

I tightened one hand on his shoulder as I let the other move up his neck and into his hair. I gripped the silky locks in my fingers, and I tugged his head back to give me better access. He moaned into my mouth before I pulled away and pressed my lips to his sharp jaw.

I followed a path down to his neck, and I let my tongue snake out like his had on me. I tasted him, the edge of salt beneath the musky taste of his body wash. He was addicting. Every single part of him, and I couldn't stop myself as I continued to kiss my way down his neck and onto his chest.

I moved against him, my body already craving more of what he had to give, and I loved the way he groaned due to what I was doing to him.

I dropped my hand from his shoulder and worked it down his body until it rested between us. He still wore his boxers, but I could feel the length of him. My hand shook slightly as I slid it beneath his boxers and my skin met his.

He dropped his head to my shoulder and let out a shuddering breath at the contact. He was so smooth and so slick, and I moved my hand back and forth between us as I tried to touch every inch of him.

My hand moved from the base of his penis to the head, and I moaned as my fist slapped against my pussy with each stroke.

"God, Josie." His breath rushed in and out against my neck, and I moved my hand just as quickly. Every time my hand hit me, I felt like I was going to break. I was still so sensitive, the feeling almost too much, but I couldn't stop.

Feeling him against me like this made me feel powerful. I had him in my hand, his pleasure mine to give, and I wanted him to want me more than he had ever wanted anyone before.

I wasn't a fool. If I hadn't already known that Beck was far more experienced than me, the way he just mastered my body on the side of the pool hammered that fact in.

I knew that he had probably been with girls who knew what the hell they were doing. I was sure that Cami knew what she was doing, but that didn't stop me.

I wasn't Cami. I wanted him and only him, and I wanted to give him more pleasure than anyone ever had before.

His teeth sank into my neck as I worked him between us, and I cried out as I felt the move all the way to my core. Beck pushed his boxers down his legs before one of his hands wrapped around mine. He followed my movements until we hit the tip, his bare skin finally touching mine, and he stopped me there.

He forced my hand along with his as he rubbed his cock up and down my pussy. I tensed as he edged toward my opening. I didn't know if I was ready for that. Not when he had been drinking, and I wasn't thinking clearly.

I wanted him. There was no doubt about that, but I also feared what he would do.

He had the power to use me any way he wanted, and I knew that his want didn't last long. If I gave myself over to him entirely, I wasn't sure that I would recover.

He would move on as if nothing had ever happened, but I wouldn't.

He slid back up, pushing the tip against my clit, and I tightened my hand around him. He continued the process over and over, he slid up and down. Up and down.

My resolve to tell him no was wavering.

One small move, and he would be inside me. One small move, and Beck would leave a mark on me that I wasn't sure he wanted to leave.

He would be my first, and even when I wanted to forget

him, I knew I never would. If I let him have that part of me, if I let him take it, I would never escape his hold on me.

But the more he rubbed against me, the more I was convinced that I would never want to escape.

"Beck." I gripped his shoulders and tightened my thighs around him as he hit my entrance again. I had no idea what I was asking for. We were in the middle of a pool, at my job, and I didn't want anything to do with him only a few moments before.

Now I was willing to give him anything.

"Please. I need more."

His hand spasmed around mine, but he didn't stop moving. He pressed harder into my clit, and I squirmed against him.

"Not tonight." His breathing was heavy, his words rushed. I hadn't expected him to turn me down. That thought hadn't even crossed my mind.

I looked away from him, but he quickly brought my mouth back to his. He kissed me like he was desperate for it. Like it was the first time our lips had touched.

"Not like this." He continued to move his hand, and I stared into his eyes as my orgasm built and built. "Not here."

"You worried I'm going to take advantage of you?" I joked, but his eyes darkened so quickly at my words that I shuddered against him.

I wasn't Cami. I hope he knew that. I hope he knew that I would never use him like that. I started to tell him that much when his mouth slammed down on mine. His hand moved faster and faster over mine, and I knew he was close.

Water splashed around us, small waves hitting us in the chest, and I tightened my hand around him.

I couldn't think as he kissed me senseless. I could barely breathe. It only took two more hard strokes of his cock against me, and I fell apart. This orgasm raking through me harder than the first.

My body felt spent, it felt like it couldn't handle another second of anything, and I gasped as he quickly pumped our hands over him.

He followed me over the edge, his cum hitting my stomach moments before it disappeared in the water, and my body slumped against his.

He held me like that for long moments without either of us saying a word, but I knew we couldn't stay here forever.

Not in this place, not in this moment, not in this imaginary bubble where everything felt right.

"We should get out of here," Beck whispered against my neck, and I nodded my head. I held on to him for a few more moments before I finally worked up the courage to let go.

We climbed out of the pool side by side, and he tossed me his dry t-shirt as he watched me. He was looking at me like I was a caged animal. Like I could break at any moment.

I thought that maybe he had felt like we had gone too far. I thought his concern was for me, but I was a fool.

I knew there would be consequences once I crossed that line with him. A line we had been tiptoeing since we met, but I hadn't realized the extent of those consequences.

I knew that Beck wouldn't be my knight in shining armor. He wasn't the end game. He was just a boy in a town that I would forget at the end of this year.

That was what I was telling myself.

Beck Clermont was forgettable.

But I was so wrong.

I would never forget Beck or the way he made me feel that night, and neither would anyone else.

CHAPTER
SEVENTEEN

L ucas had barely looked at me all day.

I knew he was probably still mad that I had left the party with Beck, and I probably should have apologized to him. But I couldn't bring myself to do it.

My father had insisted on us having a family dinner tonight, and I wanted to argue. I didn't want to sit around a table with them and fake smiles and conversation.

Especially when my mind was somewhere else.

All I could think about was Beck.

I had driven us both home last night, and we both were a mess. He was shirtless and in a pair of jeans. His t-shirt was covering my wet bra and hung to my knees. My wet hair was piled on top of my head, but I didn't care about any of that.

He held my hand in his the entire time I drove us, and I couldn't stop myself from thinking about what things could be like with him. If Beck Clermont truly wanted me, wanted me for more than just my body or some stupid revenge he planned against my stepbrother.

Beck could hate Lucas, and Lucas could hate Beck. Neither of those things stopped me from wanting him. They didn't stop my stupid heart from wanting more.

When Beck climbed out of my car, he had wrapped his hand in my hair, and he kissed me like he meant it. He kissed me like he was reminding me of something. It was like he was marking me, but even without that kiss, I would never forget.

"How's school going, Josie?" My father lifted his wine glass, and I brought my attention back to him.

"It's okay." I wasn't lying. It was less daunting than I thought it would be. Even with everyone watching and whispering about my every move.

"Lucas, how's the team looking?"

Lucas looked like he was as annoyed as I was to be here, which was weird. He always did exactly what my father asked. He was the perfect son, and perfect sons didn't grip their forks

in their hands like they were going to break them when their
father spoke to them.

"It's fine. Coach has been talking about Will Hollis again."

Will? The Will I met at the beach party?

"I'll deal with it." My father's response was quick and final.

"What's going on with Will?" I took a bite of the chicken,
and I made a mental note to thank Liz later. It was delicious.

"You know Will Hollis?" Lucas looked at me like I was crazy.

"I've met him. Yes."

"Of course, you have." Lucas chuckled, but the way he said
it didn't sit well with me at all.

"What the hell is that supposed to mean?"

"Josie, please watch your mouth at the table." I looked over
at my stepmother, and I wanted to tell her to go to hell. She
wasn't my mother, and she didn't get to act like one.

We were all quiet for a long time as we ate. I didn't have
anything to say to any of them.

I liked Lucas, but his mood swings were getting on my
nerves.

My father spoke to Lucas and me again, but I barely
responded. I just wanted to get away from them all.

By the time we finished dinner, I felt exhausted and
completely over all of them.

Amelia was still staring up at my father like he was the best
thing that had ever happened to her in her life, and I felt sorry
for her.

I pushed away from the table and asked to be excused.

My father let me go, and I felt Lucas following soon
behind me.

Lucas gripped my elbow as soon as we got to the top of the
stairs and jerked me to a stop. "What the hell are you doing
with Beck?"

"I'm not doing anything." I tried to jerk my arm from him,
but his hold was firm.

"I'm not fucking around, Josie." His eyes bounced around my face as if he thought he might find the truth there. "If you've done something, you need to tell me."

He was out of his damn mind.

We may have gotten closer since I moved here, but that didn't mean shit to me. Lucas was being an asshole, and I wouldn't allow him to treat me like this.

"What happened between the two of you?" I stepped closer to him, forcing him to adjust his hold on me. "Why do you hate him so badly? What did you do?"

"You automatically assume that I was the one who did something." He laughed, and part of me felt bad for him. He looked lost and maybe even sad. Whatever happened between him and Beck had affected him whether he wanted to admit it or not.

"Beck wouldn't—"

He cut me off as he brought his face closer to mine. I tried to back up, but he held me there, helpless against him.

For the first time since I met Lucas, I was scared of him.

"Beck wouldn't what, Josie? You don't know a damn thing about him. You have no idea what he's capable of."

I knew what he said should have worried me, but all I could think about was how badly I wanted to get to Beck. I wanted to run away from this place and into his arms.

I knew he wasn't my savior, but he was better than this.

"I know him better than you do." I jerked my arm again, and this time Lucas let it go. "I'm not some fool, Lucas. I know what I'm doing."

"Do you?" He ran his hands through his hair and stared at me. "I won't tell you again to stay away from him."

I jolted back. "You are not my father."

"No." He shook his head. "I'm not. But I'm doing what's best for you. He's using you."

I had the same thought over and over in my head, but

hearing it out loud was different. Hearing Lucas say those words felt like I was choking on them.

"You don't know that." My voice was weaker than only moments before, and I hated it. Lucas knew that he hit his mark. He knew that I cared about Beck far more than I would admit.

"I do. Clermonts and Voses don't mix. Beck hates us, Josie. He may want in between your legs, but he hates us just the same."

I reared back to slap him, but Lucas caught my hand in his before I could. He looked good and truly angry now, and I wanted his hands off me.

"Don't be his whore, Josie, because that's exactly how he'll treat you."

I jerked my hand from his and moved away from him before he could say another word. I didn't want to hear what he had to say.

I didn't believe a word that passed his lips.

Beck and I hadn't discussed anything beyond last night, but that didn't make me a whore. What happened between us was far too good to be spoiled by Lucas's words.

Even if nothing else ever came of us, if last night was all we ever amounted to, I wouldn't regret it.

And I wouldn't let Lucas make me feel like a whore for it.

I climbed down the stairs and pushed through the back door before anyone could stop me. I needed to get out of that house.

There, I was nothing but a Vos. In this town, that's all they could see. But I wasn't one of them.

I didn't hate Beck Clermont or his family, and I didn't care whether or not his father was as successful as mine.

I didn't care about anything that Lucas threatened me with.

I pushed out onto the beach and pulled fresh air into my lungs. I kicked my shoes to the side and let my toes sink into the sand. The sun was falling below the edge of the sea, and I felt like I was falling with it.

Everything felt like it was too much.

Beck, Lucas, my dad. I hadn't wanted any part of any of them, but that hadn't mattered.

I sat down on the sand just out of reach of the ocean, and I tried to concentrate on nothing but the sound of the water.

I used to do that a lot when my mom was sick. I would go outside and concentrate on something that was bigger than me. The ocean didn't care about me or my life or my inconsequential problems. It just continued to push forward, it slammed against the earth over and over as if nothing I did mattered at all.

I sat there for a long time, and every time one of them would pop into my mind, I tried to push them away. But Beck refused to let up. I concentrated on the sounds, I dug my toes into the sand, I sang "Without Me" by Halsey over and over in my head, but none of that could keep him from my thoughts.

The sun was gone by the time I finally sat up. There was nothing but the water, the moon, and me, and it reminded me how alone I was.

It didn't matter how I felt or how Beck didn't feel. Nothing in this life was permanent. Whatever did or didn't happen with him was temporary. It all was.

I pushed off the sand to stand and turned back toward the house. I stopped dead in my tracks when I saw Beck sitting there, a good twenty feet behind me, and he was just watching me.

I hadn't heard him or seen him, and I had no idea how long he had been there. He was sitting on a low wall at the edge of my property, and his hands were on his knees. His eyes, though, they were on me.

I felt awkward as I walked toward him. My hair was blowing around my face, my heart was racing, and my head was a mess.

We hadn't spoken since I left him last night, and I didn't know what to say now.

Especially after talking with Lucas.

It made me feel off. He made me second-guess everything.

I stopped when I was still a handful of feet away from him. "What are you doing out here?"

"Looking for you." He seemed distant, and I didn't know if that was just in my head. "I tried to message you."

My eyes flicked up to my house, then back to him. "I left my phone."

He nodded and looked out toward the water. "Are you okay?"

"Why wouldn't I be?" Unless he meant because of what happened last night. I didn't know why he would think I wasn't okay unless he thought I regretted it. Unless he was regretting what we had done. "Last night was amazing."

His gaze jumped back to mine, and I wanted to close the distance between us and force him to tell me what he was thinking. I wanted to kiss him senseless and drive all the thoughts racing through his head away. I wanted to chase them from mine.

"Josie, I..." He hesitated and ran his fingers through his hair. I didn't. I pushed forward and bent until my face was level with his. I gave him the slightest moment to push me away before I pressed my lips against his in a desperate kiss.

His hands found my hips and he pulled me down against him until I was straddling his lap. I groaned at the contact and the memories that were still fresh on my mind, and I kissed him like I never wanted to let him go.

His arms wrapped around my back, and he felt just as desperate. His touch was brutal and bruising and filled with so much need.

"Stay with me tonight?" His words were muffled against my mouth.

"What?"

"Stay with me." He pulled me back and looked me in the eyes. "Just for tonight. Just you and me."

"Your parents." There was no way I was just walking into his house and letting Mr. Clermont see me there. Not like this.

"They aren't home." His hand shook slightly against my back. "They won't be back until late."

"I don't know." I shook my head, but I wanted to. I wanted to be alone with him, where the rest of the world couldn't touch us.

"No expectations. We don't have to do anything. I just want you there."

My heart felt like it was going to pump out of my chest. "Okay."

He smiled up at me, the first smile I'd seen on his face since I first saw him out here, and he stood with me in his arms.

I laughed as I wrapped my legs around him. "I should go tell my dad something."

"He won't even notice you're gone." He was right, but the thought still wounded me a bit.

I wrapped my arms tighter around him as he carried me through the sand. He didn't set me down until we pushed through his back gate. He kept my hand in his as we passed the pool, and I tried not to blush. The memories of the night before came flooding back, and I was about to spend an entire night with him.

I wouldn't lie and say that thought didn't make me nervous.

He said there were no expectations, but there were. With guys like Beck, there would always be expectations. His and mine.

And I was suddenly more scared of mine than his.

Tonight, I needed him to make everything Lucas had said disappear. I just needed to feel something more. Just for one night.

I wasn't looking for a promise. I was just looking for something that only he could give me.

We pushed through the back door, leaving the cool air behind us, and it was mostly dark inside as he led me through. The house was so similar to my father's but so different at the same time. It actually looked like someone lived here.

There were dozens of photos on the walls of Beck, Frankie, his father, and his mom. They looked happy. They looked like a family.

They looked so different from us.

He led me upstairs without a word before opening a door and flicking on a lamp. The large room was shrouded in soft light, and I took in every square inch. There were some clothes thrown on the floor by his bed, which was unmade and covered in deep gray bedding. There was a desk near the window that overlooked the ocean, and I ran my fingers over the dark wood that was scattered with papers and a few baseballs.

I didn't know what to do or say. I was in his space, everything about this moment intimate, and I stared out the window to avoid looking at him.

"You want to watch a movie?" He pushed my hair over my shoulder to bare my neck to him, and he laid a gentle kiss against my skin. It shouldn't have had the impact that it did.

"Yeah."

He intertwined his fingers with mine and walked back toward his bed. My heart raced as I let him lead me. He felt different tonight. He wasn't rushed or angry or overwhelmed with need. It was just me and him, and something about that seemed far scarier than the rest.

Normally I didn't have time to think. He never allowed me room to second-guess.

He climbed onto the bed, and I followed him. He leaned against his headboard and opened his legs before he pulled me between them. My back was pressed to the front of him, and he wrapped his arms around me as he relaxed.

I was stiff as a board.

"Relax, Josie." He chuckled and grabbed a remote. "I'm not going to bite you." He nipped my ear between his teeth as soon as the lie passed his lips, and I felt the move all the way to my core.

I didn't know how he expected me to relax when he was doing things like that. There was no way in hell.

I let my body fall into his, and I pressed my thighs together to try to curb the ache he had started. We hadn't even been alone in his room for five minutes, and already that was all I could think about.

"What do you want to watch?" He was clicking through different apps, but it all felt like a blur. All I could concentrate on was the way his chest rose and fell beneath me and the way his thighs surrounded mine.

"I don't care."

He clicked on some movie I had never heard of and pressed Play before tossing the remote to the foot of the bed. I felt so hyperaware of his attention on me that I couldn't focus on a single thing that was happening on the TV.

His fingers trailed up and down my forearm. They were gentle and innocent and made me feel like I was losing my mind.

"What was your mom like?" His question was so out of the blue and so unlike him that I thought I was hearing things.

"What?" I looked over my shoulder at him, but his fingers still moved.

"Your mom. What was she like?" His eyes were soft and pleading. He looked like he truly wanted to know. Like he needed to know something real about me as desperately as I did him.

I faced back toward the TV and thought of what to say. My

mother was a million different things, and it was hard to describe her in conversation. "She was incredible." I gripped the edge of my shorts and dug my fingernails into the fabric. "She was fun and always smiling, and she always had a way to make me feel better."

"You miss her." It wasn't a question, but I nodded my head anyway.

"Like crazy." I bit down on my lip and told myself I wouldn't cry. "But I miss who she was before she got sick. That's fucked up. Isn't it?"

"That's not fucked up."

He was wrong though. I didn't regret a single moment I had with my mother, but the last few years with her had been hard. I had to watch her die a little bit every day, right before my eyes, and it ate away at me like nothing else ever would.

If I could go back, I would go back to the mom whose smile wasn't clouded with pain. I wanted her back. I desperately wanted to see her again. To feel her.

"I can't imagine what you had to go through."

We were both quiet for a moment. I didn't trust myself to say more about her. Not without crying and ruining our entire night. I wished my mom could have met Beck. She would have liked him, but she would have warned me that he was trouble.

That was what she had always said about my dad. He was handsome, but he was trouble. She knew it from the moment she met him, but it hadn't mattered. According to her, she hadn't even had time to look up before she fell. It was instant and unstoppable, and I couldn't imagine how someone like her could have ever loved someone like him.

"My dad's sick."

I turned to look at him again, but this time he tightened his arms and held me still.

"It's why I'm at the club so much. He's trying to train me to take over while he still can."

"I'm sorry, Beck. I didn't know."

His arms tightened, then loosened again as if he couldn't control it. "No one does, really. Only Olly and Carson and a few others."

"Is he going to be okay?" I asked him the question I used to hate when others asked me. As if a teenager had any idea whether or not their parent would be okay. As if we could possibly know if anything would ever be okay again.

"He thinks so. He's just getting weaker and weaker, and he hates relying on others for anything. He's a workaholic, and he's never known anything but that."

I nodded my head because I understood. My mother hated when I had to start taking things over for her. When the simplest daily task became too hard. "But he has you."

He was quiet for a long moment, then his head hit my shoulder. "I don't know that I'm enough."

I turned in his arms, forcing his arms to loosen around me. Beck Clermont was more than anyone else I had ever met.

"You are." I pressed my hand to his jaw and forced him to look up at me. He looked so lost and so broken, and I wanted to fix him. I wanted to fix every fucked-up part of him and save him from whatever destruction I knew he would cause to himself.

Because that was the only way a man like Beck could fall. Only if he cut himself off at the knees.

My lips met his, and he let me lead the kiss for the first time. I was still between his legs, our bodies pressed together, but I felt like I was miles away from him. I desperately wanted to get closer. I wanted to crush that look in his eyes and replace it with something better.

I wanted him to feel what I felt. I wanted him to see what I saw when I looked at him.

Not everyone else. Not these damn people who worshipped him but didn't see an ounce of who he really was.

I licked his bottom lip, and he opened his mouth on a groan. I deepened our kiss as I wrapped my fingers in his hair. Everything smelled like him. The room, his bed, being so close to him. He was all I could smell. He was all I could see.

I turned to get better access, and I pushed onto my knees as I kissed him harder. He was still holding back. His kiss, his hands, everything about him was being held back, and I hated it.

"Beck," I growled against his lips and felt his smile.

"This isn't why I asked you to come here." He gently pushed against my arms, but I didn't care. I turned to face him fully, and I moved my knees onto either side of his. I was fully straddling him, and our lips were only a breath apart.

"I don't care." I kissed him again, and this time he didn't hold back. One of his hands fisted in my hair as he devoured my mouth, and every part of my body came alive as he took over.

He pulled my head back by my hair, opening my neck up to him, and he kissed his way down my jaw and to the sensitive skin waiting there. My hips moved against his, and I moaned as I felt his erection beneath me.

"We should stop." He moved the strap of my tank top off my shoulder and followed the trail with his mouth.

"We shouldn't." I shook my head and focused on chasing the feeling of his body beneath mine.

"You're going to hate me tomorrow." He sounded so sure of himself. So sure of my feelings for him, but he was wrong. There was nothing he could do to make me hate him. Even if he decided that tonight was all he wanted, I still wouldn't.

I knew the score when I walked through his bedroom door. I wasn't Beck's girlfriend. I wasn't anything other than the girl who was currently on top of him, but I didn't care.

I still wanted him more than I wanted anything else.

It was irrational and crazy, and it was the only thing in my life that felt right.

"I won't."

He kissed the top of my breast before he jerked my tank top and bra down to expose me.

He stared at my breast, his mouth hovering over my sensitive skin, before looking up at me. "You fucking will."

He looked so haunted, and I wanted to stop him. But his tongue flicked against my nipple, and I couldn't think of anything but the way he sucked it into his mouth.

My back arched, pushing my breasts closer to him, and I held on to his head. My fingers pushed through his dark brown locks, and I couldn't stop watching him as he devoured me. He moved from one breast to the next, taking his time with each, and I knew that I was already dripping wet for him.

I could feel my pulse in my sex, and I felt like I was going to die if he didn't touch me. The friction of me moving against his lap wasn't enough.

I reached between us, and I tried to touch him with clumsy fingers. I wanted him out of his shorts. I wanted to see him like he had seen me last night. Nothing between us.

He pushed my hand away and laid me back on the bed. I pulled my shirt and bra over my head before he could say a word, and I continued to ride his hips in an attempt for more.

He dipped his tongue into my belly button before he flipped me over onto my stomach. I didn't know what he was doing until he ripped my shorts and panties down my legs. I looked over my shoulder and saw his shirt come off next. He was staring at my ass as he pushed his shorts down his hips. I bit my lip as he ran his hand up and down his length.

He forced me up onto my knees, and panic rushed through me. He didn't give me any time though. His tongue ran along the length of my pussy from behind, and I cried out into his comforter.

My shoulders were pressed into the bed, and I was thankful for their stability. I wasn't sure that I would have been able to hold myself up in that moment. Not with what he was doing with his mouth.

His hands were on my ass, and he spread me open as he ravaged me. There was no other word for it. That was exactly what Beck was doing. He was ravaging me like a man who was starved, and I couldn't comprehend the way he was touching me or the way my entire body tightened within moments of him starting.

I was going to come before he had even really gotten a taste of me. But I was too far gone to be embarrassed. I screamed into his bed as my orgasm racked through my body. My knees fell, but he held me upright, and he didn't stop eating me until every ounce of pleasure was pulled from my body.

I felt like I could pass out right then and there. My body completely spent, but I still wanted more of him. I pushed up on an elbow and looked back at the fucking god who sat behind me. That was what he looked like. His hair was disheveled, his chin was covered in my wetness, and the look in his eyes told me that he could do far more with my body if I would let him.

I suddenly understood why everyone worshipped him.

He was more than what I should have been allowed to have. He was more than I deserved.

I turned over in front of him, and his cock was still in his hand. I wanted him inside me.

There was no fear or hesitation.

I wanted him. I was absolutely certain.

"Beck, please." I opened my legs and looked up at him, but he wasn't as sure about me as I was him.

He moved his hand up and down his cock, and he stared at me like I was breakable. "That's not a good idea, Josie."

"Please." I was begging him as I ran my hand down my body and pressed my fingers against my still thrumming clit.

"God." He groaned and moved to his knees as he kicked his shorts from his legs. He was completely bare in front of me, and I had never seen anything more beautiful.

He rubbed his cock up and down my wetness, and he watched every inch of the movement. I squirmed against him, overwhelmed by the feel of him, and at the same time, dying for more.

"This is enough." His voice was so strained, and I knew he was holding himself back.

The thought that he didn't want to sleep with me crept its way into my head, and I felt like I couldn't breathe. He had slept with Cami. He had probably slept with those countless other girls, but he didn't want me.

I shifted beneath him, and I reached for his blanket to cover myself.

"What are you doing?" His gaze jerked up to my face, and he stopped my hands from covering myself any further. "Josie, I..."

"It's okay." My voice sounded so strained, and I hated that I was letting him see me affected.

"God, I want you." His nose pressed against my breastbone, and I tried like hell to steady my breathing and racing heart. But it was no use. He was bound to hear both, and it wouldn't matter either way. He already knew how I felt. He knew what I wanted. "I've never wanted anything more in my life."

His words were sweet, but I didn't believe them. How could I when he stood above me naked, yet refused to go any further?

"It's fine, Beck." I reached for the blanket again, but he grabbed both of my wrists and held them to the mattress above my head.

He looked like he was at war in his own head. "Promise me you won't hate me."

I didn't understand why he would keep saying that, but I made him the promise anyway. "I could never hate you, Beck."

His eyes slammed shut against my words, and he brought his mouth to mine. He kissed me hard and rushed, and I was a squirming mess beneath him. He let go of my hands long enough to grab a condom from his nightstand, and I watched him slide it on with ease.

"Are you sure?"

I nodded my head and kissed him again just as he gently pressed inside me. It hurt like hell, and I tried to breathe through the pain as he swallowed my air. He kept kissing me as my legs tensed, and I tried my hardest to focus on that and only that.

"How long has it been?" He eased out before gently moving back inside.

"How long has it been since what?" This time the pain was less but it was still there.

"Since you've had sex, Josie. You're so fucking tight."

Oh. He meant... "Never." I breathed out the word, and he came to a halt inside me.

"You're a virgin?" He sounded shocked, but I hadn't told him otherwise. I hadn't given him a reason to believe I had ever been with anyone else.

I nodded my head, and he cursed before kissing me again. He moved inside me, this time so much slower and gentler, and I found myself raising my hips to meet his as the pain eased and the pleasure began.

They were overlapping and muddled, but soon I couldn't feel anything but the way he stretched me and his hips as they ground down against my clit.

Beck started to move faster and harder when he realized I was finally chasing the pleasure he was giving me, and I was mesmerized by the way his body moved above mine. He was so handsome, so perfect, and I tugged him closer to me by the chain that hung from his neck.

His mouth met mine, and I couldn't remember where he ended and I began. Every part of me felt like it was connected to him somehow. His hands bruised me, his kiss drowned me, and his hips were making me feel like I would never come up for air.

"Tell me you're mine." He slammed his hips into mine, and I cried out against his mouth.

"I'm yours, Beck." I didn't even know what I was promising him with those simple words, but I couldn't stop them. They were the truest thing I had said all night. I would be his for however long he wanted me.

His fingers found my knees and he forced them forward as he continued to pound into me. I felt impossibly open to him, as if another simple move would break me, but he didn't care. He slammed into me over and over until something snapped inside of me and I screamed into his shoulder.

I felt like I had no control over myself. My body reeling from what he had just done, and I trembled beneath him as he slammed into me two more times before groaning my name against my neck.

We lay there like that for a long time with him holding his weight on his elbows. Neither of us said a word until he slid out of me and pressed a kiss to my belly.

"Are you okay?"

I blinked sleepy eyes at him and nodded my head. I was more than okay. I felt perfectly happy in that moment, and I wasn't sure that anything could bring me down.

I watched Beck dispose of the condom as I struggled to stay awake, and I moaned softly as he climbed back into bed and curled his body around mine. He pulled the blanket over us and clicked off the light.

I could feel him breathing behind me, his body still not

having calmed down, but I couldn't fight the pull of sleep. I was exhausted, and I felt so safe in his arms.

He kissed the back of my head as he laid his head on the pillow. "Don't forget, Josie. Don't forget what you said."

I nodded my head. "I won't."

CHAPTER
EIGHTEEN

As soon as I opened my eyes, I knew something wasn't right.

Josie was no longer in my arms. Instead, she was storming around my room, grabbing her clothes off the floor, and tugging them on in a rush.

"What are you doing?" I asked and her bloodshot eyes snapped to mine.

Something was seriously wrong.

"How dare you!" She tugged her shirt over her head, not worrying about a bra, before she tugged on her shorts.

"What's wrong?" I jumped out of the bed and pulled my own shorts on before she bolted. There was no way that she knew about what I had sent to Lucas. She didn't have her phone, and every part of me believed the coward would keep his mouth fucking shut even though I slammed it in his face.

Even though I sent him proof of me touching his sister in all the ways I knew would piss him off. I didn't get to say another word about what he did to Frankie, but I had been willing to throw what I had done to Josie in his face.

What he had done to my sister had been sent out for all his fucking friends to see, but mine had been just for him.

It was a decision that I regretted. One that I couldn't take back.

But there was no way in hell that she knew.

She stormed past me and picked up my phone off my nightstand. She threw it at my chest without saying a word, and I scrambled to catch it.

Notification after notification lit up my phone, and there in the middle of the screen was the video I had sent her brother.

"Josie, let me explain."

"Let you explain!" she screamed, and I knew that everyone in the house could hear her. My dad, my mom, and worst of all, Frankie. "What the fuck do you think there is to explain?"

I clicked on the screen and saw the video had been posted

to Instagram. Right there for everyone to see was me eating Josie while she was spread out before me on the side of the pool.

"I didn't post this." I was grasping at straws, but I had to make her understand.

"I don't believe you, Clermont."

I hated that she called me by my last name. She only did that when she hated me.

"I don't believe a damn word you say."

"I sent it to Lucas." I had no intention of telling her the truth, but it was the only thing I had. I didn't expect Lucas to send it out to anyone, let alone where the whole damn school could see. I was a fool for thinking that piece of trash had any sort of morals, but I was no better than him.

I knew that.

I wanted to destroy Lucas, but I had become just like him.

"So, you're some sort of saint?" she screamed at me, and I had never seen her so angry before. I reached for her hand, and she jerked away from me so fast it felt like she hit me. "What did I do to you?"

She didn't wait for an answer. Her voice broke as she screamed. "What the fuck did I do to deserve this?"

My hands shook at my sides, and I was dying to touch her, to hold her against me and refuse to let her go until I could explain.

I had no intentions of falling for Lucas Vos's sister.

That was never part of the plan, but as I stood there and watched the first few tears roll down her cheeks, I knew that I was a complete and total idiot.

All while I was trying to ruin every piece of her, I was slowly falling for her. And she had given me the power to do so. She handed me the power to either destroy or love her, and I showed her exactly who I was.

I showed her exactly what I was capable of.

"You don't deserve this."

"Then why?"

"Because of what he did to Frankie," I yelled back at her. "Don't act like you don't know what he did to her. There's no way you can be that fucking dense."

She jolted back, and I hated myself more. I was doing nothing but pushing her farther away.

This was exactly what he wanted.

This was exactly why he had posted this. He knew that I would ruin myself.

"What are you talking about?"

"Your brother, Josie. He..." I ran my hands through my hair because I could barely breathe, let alone think. "He fucking assaulted her."

She looked like she was going to be sick, but I couldn't stop now. I hadn't talked about what happened with anyone since those few weeks after it happened when everything was swept under the rug.

"He and his friends assaulted her, and one of their buddies recorded it. He was my friend." I slammed my hand into my chest. "He was my friend, and she was in love with him. She had been for years, and he fucking broke her."

She searched my face for the truth, but I had already obliterated every bit of trust she had in me.

"So, you decided to break me?"

"No." I shook my head, but she was right. That was exactly what I was doing.

"You made me fall for you, then you fucking crushed me."

"You didn't fall for me."

"No." She backed away from me until her hand was gripping the doorframe. "I can't believe I was so stupid."

"Josie." Her name had barely passed my lips when the door suddenly opened, and our fathers and Lucas pushed through the door with panic on their faces.

It was clear from the look of us what had happened here last night.

"What the hell is going on here?" Mr. Vos was furious, and I should have been happy. That was what I wanted all along. To smear his name. To make him feel like we had felt.

I didn't give a shit about him right now though. I only cared about Josie, and how big of a damn idiot I had been.

Lucas moved to her side, and every part of me wanted to pummel him. I wanted to wrap my hands around his neck and watch the fucking life leave his eyes. He had taken so much from me, and this was just another move for him.

I should have known that he wouldn't fucking care about her. That doing this to his sister wouldn't hurt him the way he had hurt me. He didn't care about anyone but himself.

I stepped forward, my body vibrating with anger, but Josie stopped me in my tracks.

She moved toward him, and he wrapped his arms around her as she cried. I wanted to rip her from his touch.

My stomach rolled, and I couldn't stop myself. I couldn't just let her fall into his arms like he was somehow going to protect her from me.

As if he was the damn hero.

I had been every bit the villain she thought I was, but I still wasn't him.

I was just the guy who pushed her straight into his arms.

"Josie." I reached for her, but Lucas tucked her tighter against him. She wasn't even looking at me. She couldn't see me through her anger and sadness.

"Please, Josie." I just needed to talk to her. I needed to make her understand.

"I think you've done enough, Beck."

"Are you really speaking to me right now?" I stepped forward, to do what, I didn't know. He held her between us. He was using her as a barrier because he knew I wouldn't harm her. Not physically, at least.

I had harmed her enough already.

"Beck, back off." This was from my father. I looked up at him, and I had never seen such disappointment in his face. He was looking at me the same way he was looking at Lucas, and I wanted to scream.

"Take me home," she whispered to Lucas as her fingers dug into his shirt.

I couldn't stand another moment of it. I reached out and touched her shoulder as I said her name again. She startled as if she was burned by just my touch.

And she had been.

I had set fire to everything that we were, everything that we could have been, with the hopes of destroying her family. But the only thing I managed to destroy was her. I destroyed her and my own damn heart at the exact same time.

I was nothing but the villain and had no chance of ever getting her back.

Not after what I'd done.

"That trash account has been taken down." Her father's voice shook against the walls. "But the damage has already been done."

"Let's not pretend we haven't been here before." I pushed my hair out of my face, and I should have kept my mouth shut.

"Beckham." My father's voice boomed as he stood in front of me and blocked my view of her. "That's enough."

"But did you notice in this video that Josie was awake? Did you notice that she hadn't had enough alcohol to kill her?"

My father slammed his hands into my chest, and I stumbled back, shocked. My father had never put his hands on me.

Lucas pulled Josie from the room, his arms still around her, and panic was taking over every part of me.

If he took her with him, I would never make her understand. She would fucking hate me. It was what I had thought I wanted, but I was wrong.

"Josie."

She looked up at me, and the look on her face devastated me. I had broken her. This room was full of men who had done so much wrong, and she was the one who had ended up hurt.

She was the only one that mattered.

"You stay the fuck away from my daughter." Joseph Vos had the nerve to point his finger in my direction like he hadn't just let her walk out of the room with a monster.

"I won't." I shook my head, and my father huffed as if he couldn't believe me.

But neither one of them could keep me from her. It didn't matter that she hated me. I would get her to listen to me.

I had to.

The thought of her walking away now, of me fucking this up so damn badly, it was too much to bear.

I couldn't deal with her hating me. I couldn't handle the look on her face.

Josie Vos was mine, whether she still felt the same way or not, and I wouldn't stop until I had her.

to be continued

JOSIE AND BECK'S
STORY CONTINUES IN
THE FALL OF A GOD
COMING JUNE 10TH, 2021.

THANK YOU

Thank you so much for reading Josie and Beck's story! Their story will continue in The Fall of a God, and I cannot wait for you all to read more of this dynamic couple.

I would love for you to join my reader group, Hollywood, so we can connect and talk about all of your The Touch of Villain thoughts. This group is the first place to find out about cover reveals, book news, and new releases!

Join us for the fun:
www.facebook.com/groups/hollyrenee

You can also sign up for my newsletter here:
www.authorhollyrenee.com/subscribe

ACKNOWLEDGMENTS

Thank you for taking a chance on reading this book!

I owe so many thanks to every blogger, bookstagrammer, and reader who shares, reads, reviews, and loves my books. I will never be able to express my gratitude.

I have so many people to thank for having my back and being a part of the best team ever.

I would like to think my wonderful family for always being so supportive and encouraging my dreams.

A big thanks to my beta team, Megan, Katie, Rita, Aundi, Heather, Elizabeth, and Christina. This book would be nothing without you all.

Thank you to Christina Santos who keeps me sane and feels like the backbone of my support. I will never be able to tell you how much I appreciate you!

Thank you to Jen at Wildfire for how hard you work for me and how much you support me. I will be forever grateful for you.

To Becca, Ellie, and Rumi, thank you for helping me turn this book into what it is.

To my author friends who keep me sane and pushing forward every day. I love you all.

And to the best street team ever, thank you for everything you all do! I am so thankful for you all!

Printed in Great Britain
by Amazon

79301789R00188